Sherlock Holmes
and the
Apocalypse Murders

Center Point
Large Print

Also by Barry Day and available from
Center Point Large Print:

*Sherlock Holmes and the
    Shakespeare Globe Murders*
*Sherlock Holmes and the
    Alice in Wonderland Murders*
*Sherlock Holmes and the
    Copycat Murders*

SHERLOCK HOLMES
and the
Apocalypse Murders

BARRY DAY

CENTER POINT LARGE PRINT
THORNDIKE, MAINE

The text of this Large Print edition is unabridged.
In other aspects, this book may vary
from the original edition.
Printed in the United States of America
on permanent paper.
Set in 16-point Times New Roman type.

ISBN: 978-1-68324-472-1

Library of Congress Cataloging-in-Publication Data

Names: Day, Barry, author.
Title: Sherlock Holmes and the apocalypse murders / Barry Day.
Description: Center Point Large Print edition. | Thorndike, Maine :
Center Point Large Print, 2017.
Identifiers: LCCN 2017022039 | ISBN 9781683244721
     (hardcover : alk. paper)
Subjects: LCSH: Holmes, Sherlock—Fiction. | Watson, John H.
(Fictitious character)—Fiction. | Private investigators—England—
Fiction. | Murder—Investigation—Fiction. | Large type books. | GSAFD:
Mystery fiction.
Classification: LCC PR6054.A928 S5424 2017 | DDC 823/.914—dc23
LC record available at https://lccn.loc.gov/2017022039

This one is for
LYNNE . . .
(. . . not forgetting OSCAR)

CHAPTER ONE

ey, Inspector, talk about somebody wearing
heart on their sleeve . . . !"

strade, if your officer has nothing more
ful to contribute, I really think . . ."

quite right, Mr. 'Olmes. You get off and
t interviewing the neighbours and see if
ybody heard anything. Mind you . . ."—and
turned towards Sherlock Holmes—"if the last
t's anything to go by . . . Sorry about young
cLinsky . . ."—this to the departing back of the
eepish police constable—"he's a good lad but
bit quick with the tongue, if you know what I
mean. Comes from having a Scots father and a
Russian mother, I shouldn't wonder. Why, when I
was on the beat . . ."

"Quite, Lestrade, quite," said Holmes, cutting
off what promised to be an endless biographical
anecdote. "Now, what have we here that you
considered important enough that Dr. Watson and
I had to interrupt our dinner?"

I was wondering precisely the same thing, as
we stood shivering in our thin evening clothes
in a poorly-lit mews not far from Oxford Circus
but a world away from the bustling atmosphere
of our favourite watering-hole, Simpson's-in-the-
Strand.

Earlier that evening—in late January 1895, according to my notes of the case—Holmes had proposed the outing. For the past three days he had spent every waking moment hunched over his deal-topped table in the corner of our sitting room, cooking up one malodorous compound after another, until on the very stroke of six he had raised a triumphant test tube aloft, as though he were about to give a toast—which in a way it turned out that he was.

"This, my dear Watson, will hang the third most dangerous man in England and the cleverest poisoner who has ever crossed my path. I can now prove how he tampered with the Oppenshaws' poached eggs without breaking the skin. When you come to record it, you may wish to call it something like 'The Affair of the Locked Egg'—but it is not for me to interfere in literary matters . . ."

I muttered something I hoped was incomprehensible from behind the *Evening Standard*. Holmes's teasing about my chronicling of his cases was inclined to be increasingly heavy-handed and I could not help but feel that there was a tinge of jealousy about the reputation I was beginning to enjoy. Why, only this morning . . .

". . . and your latest royalty cheque seems to have exceeded your expectations . . ."

"But how . . . ?" I said, before I realised that I had once more fallen into his trap.

"My dear Watson, we are given features to express our emotions and yours are an open book. Mrs. Hudson brought you three letters this morning. The first was clearly an advertising circular, since you tore it up unread. The second in a buff envelope was equally a bill of some sort, which you hastily pushed behind the toast rack. The third you opened in considerable haste and immediately beamed—rather smugly, I might add—from ear to ear. You next took a pencil, retrieved a portion of the torn envelope and jotted down a number with three figures in it. From which I deduce that you were examining your royalty statement and that it was more than the £93.5s.9d. you received the last time.

"After which you did something that totally convinced me that I was not in error . . ."

"And that was . . . ?"

"You fetched *The Sporting Life* from your overcoat pocket and began making those enthusiastic but invariably abortive hieroglyphics on it. You were in funds. Capital, Watson, capital. So we both have something to celebrate. You may keep your ill-gotten gains. Tonight the treat is on me. Would a little something nutritious at Simpson's suffice?"

"It would, indeed."

And so we were cosily ensconced when the *mâitre d'* hove into view to tell us that a police constable needed to see us urgently with a message from Inspector Lestrade. Holmes and I exchanged glances over the succulent rare steaks we had just that moment been served. I had been picturing them in my mind since he had made the suggestion and I could just visualise my knife poised for that first incision . . .

But right now I was doing my very best to banish the thought, as I watched my friend bend to examine what we "had here."

Croxley Mews, W.1. was a secluded spot, to say the least—one of those typical London backwaters that exist only a very few paces from a major artery, yet one could and did pass it day by day without even knowing it was there. Yet tonight someone had found it who would not be leaving.

At the very end of the mews was a Georgian house, shuttered and deserted—except for what lay at the bottom of the "area" steps. As I peered over the railings, I could see Holmes and Lestrade bent over the body of a stout, middle-aged woman. Then, as Lestrade straightened up that whippet-like frame of his, I suddenly saw what had prompted McLinsky's inopportune remark. At that moment I could wish that I had been back at Simpson's ordering the fish—for not only was it clear that the unfortunate lady lying so immodestly on that filthy paving had been brutally murdered but whoever had killed her had removed several internal organs and arranged them carefully on top of her body.

In the course of my medical career I had seen some horrific sights, particularly in the field of battle, but never could I recall something which sent such a chill of horror through my veins as the sight of that art directed obscenity.

"Holmes!" I cried. "There's been nothing like this since . . ."

But before I could say more, he was beckoning me to join him beside the body—which, with only the slightest hesitation, I did.

"Watson, I beg you to say as little as possible until we return to Baker Street, for reasons I will explain later," he said in a tone that only Lestrade and myself could hear without it carrying to the knot of police standing at the top of the steps to keep the inevitable onlookers at a safe distance.

"Before Lestrade has his men remove the body, I would call your attention, gentlemen, to two things. Despite being taken by surprise, the victim being a substantial lady, gave a good account of herself and managed to secure a token . . ."

And he held up a single long blonde hair. "This was caught in a fingernail. And here . . ." With that he gently lifted the woman's averted head and I could see the throat was neatly cut. In life she must undoubtedly have been a woman of strength and purpose, for the face was well-fleshed with a minimum of make-up carefully applied. In death, however, she looked defeated. It has never ceased to depress me that all the knowledge, memories and wisdom that it takes a lifetime to accumulate can be snuffed out literally in an instant.

Then I saw what Holmes was indicating. There, just below the angle of the chin, was a tiny additional "x" cut into the flesh, so gently that it had hardly bled at all.

I heard Lestrade say—"He might as well have signed his blooming name, eh, Mr. 'Olmes."

"I think he did, Lestrade. I think he just did," Holmes murmured, almost to himself, as he let the tired head rest back on the ground.

CHAPTER TWO

"But, Holmes, I had no idea . . ."

"There was no reason you should and very many good reasons why you should *not,* old fellow. The business of the so-called 'Jack the Ripper' killings was one of the most disturbing I have ever been associated with and caused me more heart searching than you can possibly imagine . . . and you of all people are not deficient in that department."

We were back in Baker Street, where Mrs. Hudson, as if anticipating our needs, had banked up a substantial fire. I had exchanged my dinner jacket for a smoker and Holmes for his favourite mouse-coloured dressing gown. That and the old clay pipe told me that he expected to be in for a long night of contemplation.

As we sat in our familiar positions on either side of the fire, I observed that Holmes was staring into and beyond the dancing light of the burning coals, as if he were seeing visions that disturbed him. As so often, I was his necessary audience, so that he could empty his mind.

"Even when the murders started back in August of 1888, I think I may say that I had acquired a certain reputation in my field . . ."

I nodded firmly but I doubt that he saw it in the dimness of the room.

". . . many people expected Scotland Yard, who were clearly baffled—as they so often are—to send for me right away when Mary Ann Nichols was killed on—I believe, August 31st. And then, when Annie Chapman was butchered on September 8th and there was still no sign of my involvement, you will remember that the popular press began to make an issue of it. I remember you even commented on it yourself?"

"I did, indeed," I replied. "It was a national disgrace."

"But you see, I *was* called in," Holmes said simply, "though not by Scotland Yard."

"I don't understand . . ."

"It was my brother Mycroft, at the behest of the very highest in the land. And on the strict understanding that my presence and anything I might discover was to be kept completely secret. I was to report only to him. As you can well imagine, Watson, such conditions went very much against the grain with me but I was given no choice in the matter . . ."

"But these were not high born women. I don't mean that the way it sounds—well, you know what I mean, Holmes . . ."

My friend continued to peer into the flames, as though he were looking back down the years.

"Mary Ann Nichols . . . Annie Chapman . . . Elizabeth Stride . . . Catharine Eddowes . . . Mary Jane Kelly . . . and perhaps others we were never sure of . . .

"You're quite right, old fellow. By no means 'ladies'—except of the street in some cases. Pathetic creatures . . . but with the God-given right to life that somebody, playing God, decided to take from them without even knowing them. But, you see, it wasn't the *victims* that concerned those in high places, though I exempt Mycroft from that callousness . . ."

"Then what was it?"

"The murderer."

"The *murderer?*"

"The powers-that-be had reason to believe that the killer was one of their own. And they look after their own. Of course, once they found him and his crimes could be proved, he would necessarily be punished—but discreetly. Out of the public gaze. One must never disturb the Great British Public—or frighten the horses."

There was a bitter tone in his voice as he continued . . .

"As those two months of ritual bloodletting went on, a clear pattern began to emerge. The man's psychology was progressively unravelling. Each crime was more savage and yet more indulgent than the last. It was as though he wanted to show that he was a conjuror who could

17

out-perform each trick with the next and hold his audience spellbound . . ."

"He certainly achieved that. The papers talked of nothing else."

"He knew the Whitechapel area intimately and had his escape routes well worked out. There were no credible reports of a 'toff' running through those crowded streets covered in blood . . ."

"As he must have been. From what I read . . ."

Holmes continued, as though I had not spoken . . .

"The man had some medical knowledge. The eviscerations were not the work of some amateur butcher and yet they fell some way short of the work of a professional surgeon . . . To cut a long story short, Watson, I took their confounded list and started there . . ."

"There was some talk at the club that there was a Royal name on it . . ."

"Oh, young Albert Victor, the Duke of Clarence? Heir apparent, if and when our beloved Prince of Wales ever does succeed to the throne? Yes, someone had thought fit to add his name in what I can only suppose was a joke in doubtful taste. Apart from the fact that he had unbreakable alibis for each of the nights in question, the young man—sadly, no long with us—was, shall we say, intellectually negligible. It was as much as he could do to cut up a grouse after the Glorious Twelfth. No, though the yellow press would have had a field day, I'm afraid the putative Prince was never—as you gambling men would say—a runner."

"Then who . . . ?"

"As to that, old fellow, I'm afraid I am still bound by that earlier promise. All I can tell you is that I approached the matter in my accustomed manner, as you would expect. That is to say, I tried to sweep my mind clear of any preconceptions and assess what little evidence there was.

"Fortunately—or, I should say, *un*fortunately—I was being presented with evidence on a dis-tressingly regular basis. Then, when I had weighed it and eliminated the impossible, what remained . . . but you of all people know my favourite axiom . . ."

"So you came to the truth?"

"And like so many mysteries, once one had solved it, the answer was obvious. And that was where the real problem started. For the man in question did indeed walk tall in the corridors of power."

"And he was allowed to walk away?"

"I'm afraid he was, Watson. You may remember that hundreds of extra police were moved into the Whitechapel area when the crimes were at their height? You may or may not know that within days—immediately after I had made my report, to be precise—they were removed overnight, much to the public's dismay."

"And wasn't there some fuss over the Police Commissioner resigning?"

"Sir Charles Warren? Yes, though it was hardly his fault. The man was incompetent and our friends needed a visible diversion. The whole thing was poorly handled throughout—except in the efficient way some of the files subsequently disappeared, so that the truth could never be proved."

"No,"—and he gave the fire a savage prod with the poker, so that the new flames lit his face from below like some embittered Mephistopheles—"It was far from my finest hour, Watson, but it was one which I hoped I had put behind me. Until tonight . . ."

"Yes, what *was* all that about, pray?"

"Lestrade was the one person in the force who was allowed to know of my involvement—I suppose it was known that we had worked together over the years with a degree of accord . . ."

I thought back to some of the things I had heard Holmes say about the Inspector's competence or, rather, lack of it but I said nothing so as not to interrupt his flow.

"We would meet privately and he would pass on such information as the Yard did have and arrange for me to see the bodies with no one else present. Neither of us has spoken of it from that day to this but when he found himself faced with a murder that brought back those dire memories, it was a matter of instinct, I suppose, to send for me. What happened tonight was the very thing that was not *supposed* to happen . . ."

"But how was that to be expected?" I interrupted. "When a man has killed once—and this man has killed several times—sure there is a bloodlust at work? He is clearly mad!"

"That I had ascertained quite early in the piece, you may be sure, Watson. Clinically demented and incredibly clever, as such people often are. For several weeks he kept the police on the hop and left barely a clue. He had the ability to appear and disappear in crowded streets. He was several times glimpsed but never clearly seen and he had the nerve to telegraph what he was doing. And even when I had unmasked him to the authorities—as I say—nothing could be done . . ."

"Nothing?"

"Next to nothing. Because of the distinguished position he held, he was taken before the Home Secretary of the day—I believe the Prime Minister was so sickened by the man's crimes that he could not bring himself to attend.

"The Home Secretary there and then ordered a special jury of his peers to hear the evidence and come to a verdict. A highly unorthodox procedure, as you will observe, but one designed to save many people from the scandal an ordinary trial would have created. Even I never knew who they were."

"And, of course, he was found guilty?"

"He was found guilty—the verdict was quite unanimous—and literally banished. He was stripped of all his honours, taken under guard to an unknown European destination and told he must never return to England. And that was supposed to be the last we should hear of 'Jack the Ripper.' Oh, what fools these mortals be, Watson. What fools . . ."

"But even supposing the Ripper *is* back, Holmes, there are things about this evening that still don't make sense. For one, this man, you say, was well known. He's bound to be recognised . . ."

"Oh, I don't suppose for one moment our friend looks remotely like he did when he was escorted under Her Majesty's pleasure. No, I think we can safely assume that aspect has been taken care of. If *I* can pass myself off with some success as an amiable old clergyman or an out of work groom, I don't think a clever man with a burning *reason* to disguise himself can't do the same. I will lay odds that we could pass this gentleman in the street this very night and be none the wiser. But that's not what worries me the most . . ."

"Then what does?"

"The man has changed his *modus operandi* and that is always of concern. His previous

22

victims were all ladies of a certain kind, pathetic creatures living in the half-light. The popular theory—with which I agreed in part—was that this man was attracted to women but at the same time feared them. Killing these 'token' women—and in such a bestial manner—was his revenge on the sex as a whole . . ."

"But it was a woman he killed tonight," I interjected. "So where is the difference?"

"Yes, old fellow, but this was a totally different kind of woman, killed in a completely different environment—the supposedly safe West End of this fashionable metropolis of ours. She was older, well-dressed—dare one say 'matronly'? Yet he treated her just like the rest. Which is why I say that he has decided to extend his range—and he wants us to know it. Hence the 'signature.' Each of the previous victims bore the 'sign of the cross.' And *that* I find distinctly concerning. Why, Watson, *why?*"

"Did you notice anything unusual about the woman, Holmes?"

"Beyond the fact that she was well-to-do, yet she was used to walking a great deal and that she had recently been performing a clerical function at which she was poorly skilled, I could deduce nothing. Oh, and, of course, that she was astigmatic and vain about the fact."

"But what led you to those conclusions?"

"The astigmatism was obvious. Those twin

indentations on either side of the nose invariably indicate the wearing of *pince-nez*, which many people seem to favour over ordinary spectacles, since they convey something of an occasional rather than a permanent necessity. As I say—female vanity. Her clothes, though not fashionable, were expensive and entirely in keeping with a woman of means, as was her whole appearance. Yet the shoes she was wearing, though obviously hers, had seen better days. Therefore, she was expecting to do a lot of walking and was wearing an old pair for comfort and not appearance. She was clearly on a practical rather than a social mission. Her hands were well-kept and carefully manicured, yet there were dozens of tiny cuts and scratches on her fingers which, I would infer, were caused by handling paper carelessly and receiving those slight but painful paper cuts that typists and secretaries are heir to. What her purpose was, I have not the slightest idea, except that it was patently important to her. But again I say—why did he choose *her?*"

Before I could answer—and I confess my mind was a complete blank—there was a knock on the sitting-room door and Mrs. Hudson came into the room in her usual unobtrusive fashion. Holmes and I had been so engrossed that we had failed to hear the clanging of the bell—the sound that had so often been the cue for another entrance on our little stage and a call to arms.

"Inspector Lestrade and another officer, Mr. Holmes. I thought it would be all right to bring him straight up?"

"Quite right, Mrs. Hudson. Come in, Lestrade—and you, too—McLinsky, isn't it?"

The young constable—obviously still conscious of his earlier *faux-pas*—seemed to be hovering in Lestrade's shadow for protection.

"Come, Watson, make room for our guests by the fire. And since by the time of night I deduce we are all off duty, perhaps a whisky and soda all round might not come amiss after the evening we've had."

"Very kind of you, Mr. 'Olmes," replied the Inspector, placing his bowler and overcoat, both of which had seen better days, rather precariously on a chair already piled high with newspapers which were awaiting Holmes's erratic filing practices.

And then, peremptorily—"You can use the ottoman, McLinsky."

I had the distinct impression Lestrade was anxious to impress his junior with the fact that 221B was a second home to him.

"Thought I'd just drop in, like, to apprise you of our latest findings, gentlemen," he went on, accepting the drink Holmes had prepared for him. "And McLinsky here has talked to people who were in the vicinity at the time." McLinsky looked suitably important.

"The victim," Lestrade went on, consulting his notebook, "was a Mrs. Adeline Hatton of 20 Eaton Square . . ."

"Adeline Hatton, founder of The Daughters of Eve." Holmes interrupted him in full flow. "Watson, be a good fellow, make a long arm and reach me volume H on the shelf behind you. Let us test the efficiency of my filing system."

When the heavy tome was on his knees, he began to riffle through it happily, being constantly diverted by what he found there.

"Good old index! What a compendium of the criminal and the bizarre—and the bizarrely criminal. The Hapsburg rubies . . . why the Austrian police couldn't solve such an absurdly simple case themselves, I'll never know . . . Here's the case of Harwood and the Hampshire Horror. Remember, Watson, that was the time we nearly lost you to a ferret infected with bubonic plague . . . ? Hastings—ingenious fellow who poisoned his wife by tampering with her lipstick . . . ah, here we are . . .

HATTON, Adeline (*née* Monteith). Born . . . I don't think we'll go into all that out of respect for the departed lady. Let us say she was of middle years. Educated at . . . etc., etc. Married Sir Arthur Hatton, K.B.E. in 1870. Two daughters, etc., etc. Now some newspaper cuttings . . . Mrs. Hatton has been concerned for many years with the issue of female suffrage and in pursuit of her work in this field, refused to adopt her husband's title, except on state occasions . . . Now, that *is* unusual, gentlemen. Not using a title is comparable to not wearing a pearl necklace, when a woman possesses either."

He continued reading. "Soon after her marriage, Lady Hatton . . .—I see *The Times* insists on protocol, even if Mrs. Hatton chose to shun it—'Lady Hatton founded The Daughters of Eve, an organisation devoted exclusively to issues affecting women. Within a few years it had grown to become a significant social force . . .' "

"I should just say it did," I added. "Do you remember that rally in Trafalgar Square a year or two back, when several of them chained themselves to Nelson's Column? I remember the *Telegraph* had an article with the headline—NELSON TURNS A BLIND EYE. Dashed good piece it was, too . . ."

"The Daughters now has a membership of . . . and so on, and so on. Lady Hatton is the author of several seminal works including: *The Primal Sin* (1888); *Prima Inter Pares* (1890) and the controversial *Women, Beware Women* (1894) . . . An articulate lady—or should I say . . . woman?"

He shut the book with a snap and placed it on the floor by his feet.

"So by striking at this *one* woman our friend is symbolically striking at *all* women. Is that it? Surely there is more to it than that?"

"McLinsky, tell Mr. Holmes and Dr. Watson about your interviews." Lestrade spoke to fill the silence that had fallen on the firelit room.

The young constable busied himself with the pages of his notebook. From where I sat I could not fail to admire the neat copperplate hand that I had struggled so hard to master at school.

"It seems that Lady—I mean 'Mrs.'—Hatton had been delivering a number of pamphlets around the area concerning a forthcoming feminist rally at Caxton Hall . . ."

"At that time of night and on foot?" I expostulated.

"Seems the lady was very independent, you might say, Doctor. She made it a rule in her organisation never to ask anyone to do anything she was not willing to do herself, down to filling envelopes . . ."

"The paper cuts," Holmes murmured in my direction.

". . . and pushing them through letterboxes. 'I abhor and eschew social privilege,' she was apparently very fond of saying. I remember reading an interview . . ."

"Get on with it, McLinsky," Lestrade interrupted testily, "we haven't got all night."

"Several people in the neighbourhood remember seeing her earlier. Someone said she looked like a galleon in full sail . . ." McLinsky consulted his notes. "But nobody can recall seeing her go in the mews. It's not very well lit at night and few people have any reason to go there . . ."

"Except her killer," said Holmes thoughtfully.

"Except, as you say, Mr. Holmes, her killer. He must have been waiting for her but how would he know . . . ?"

"Oh, I think we can assume he knew a *great* deal about her. Unless I miss my guess, he's been studying her for years."

"*Years?*" This from Lestrade. "Oh, I . . ."

But Holmes cut him off before he could continue. "The body has been positively identified, of course?"

"No doubt about that, I'm afraid, Mr. 'Olmes. We couldn't locate Sir Arthur—he was up north on a speaking engagement. Something about 'Traditional Tory Family Values,' I'm told. But we did manage to get hold of the lady's associate, a woman called—what was her name again, McLinsky?"

Another flick through the neat notebook.

"Pankhurst, sir. Mrs. Emmeline Pankhurst. Very distraught, she was, but not so much as a tear. Said something about the battle being joined when she left—whatever that's supposed to mean."

"Mark my words, gentlemen, we can expect to hear from that lady again," said Holmes. "Women are on the march and heaven help the man who stands in their way."

"You really take this 'Votes for Women' business seriously, then, Holmes?" I asked.

"So seriously, old fellow, that, should a crisis be reached, we men may well have to deploy our ultimate weapon . . ."

"Which is . . . ?"

"Your good self, Watson." He turned to Lestrade and McLinsky. "The fair sex is Watson's department. You may not be aware of it but his exploits across three continents would put my puny adventures to shame. It was only *three* continents, was it not, Watson? Or should one say two-and-a-half, since India is only a *sub*-continent?"

That foolish—and, I might add, grossly exaggerated—boast of mine in an idle moment, probably when the Beaune was doing the talking, was a constant source of amusement to Holmes. Occasionally it caused me to wonder whether his sense of humour was as well developed as some of his other skills. Nonetheless, it certainly relaxed the tension in the room, as Holmes knew it would, and for that I was grateful.

Then—as was so often the case—his mood changed. He fixed McLinsky with a penetrating stare.

"I believe there was one other matter to which you wished to draw my attention?"

Flustered, the young man searched through his notes.

"Oh, yes, one chap said he heard somebody whistling a funny little tune and then there was a loud metallic noise, like some sort of door closing. He whistled it to me and it sounded sort of familiar."

Holmes leapt to his feet, crossed to the corner of the room and picked up his violin, which was leaning there. Putting it to his chin, he asked— "Did it sound like *this* . . . ?"—and played six notes.

"But Holmes," I cried, "surely that's that little French song we used to sing when we were children? How does it go?"

And then followed the bizarre spectacle of my singing to Holmes's accompaniment . . .

Auprès de ma blonde,
J'y passerai, passerai, passerai.
Auprès de ma blonde
J'y passerai toute ma vie

"Quite right, Watson. Generally considered to be a traditional French air but, in fact, composed for the Dutch landings in Vendée in 1672. Called at one time *Le Prisonnier de Hollande* . . .

"Oh don't look so surprised, old fellow. I had cause to do my research on this very song some time ago. You are quite right, though. It has come to be thought of as a kind of *louche* nursery rhyme and to mean that one would like to spend

31

the rest of one's life in the company of a certain blonde lady companion."

At which point I intercepted an exchange of glances between Holmes and Lestrade. So the tune was another link with the past?

"Well, that's about it for tonight, gents." Lestrade got to his feet, followed a split second later by his cohort, and retrieved his coat and hat.

"Perhaps you and I should have a quiet word in the morning about—the other business . . ."

". . . about which I have seen fit to inform Dr. Watson," Holmes interjected.

It seemed to me—and I was pleased to think— that the Inspector looked distinctly relieved. The complexities of future coded communication had clearly been exercising him. It would henceforth be business as usual for all three of us—*whatever* the business turned out to be.

" 'Welcome aboard,' as they say, Doctor," said Lestrade, shaking me firmly by the hand. "I hope you can help us see a bit of daylight, because, I tell you frankly, gentlemen, right now I feel I'm in a . . ."

"*Cul-de-sac*?" suggested my friend.

A moment later they were gone and we heard the downstairs door close behind them.

CHAPTER THREE

When I came down to breakfast next morning, it was obvious that Holmes had been up for some time. The toast crumbs on his dressing gown and the litter of morning papers all round his chair left room for no other deduction.

"Holmes," I said, when I had demolished a couple of boiled eggs and poured myself a second cup of tea, "it may well be that I am a little slow off the mark, as you are frequently suggesting in your subtle way, but there are still some things about last evening that I fail to understand. For instance, what was the significance of the tune? I realised that you didn't want to elaborate in front of McLinsky . . ."

"My apologies, old fellow." Holmes looked up from his reading. "Having come so far, it is unfair of me not to place all the information before you, such as it is.

"When I identified the music so readily, it was not an act of mind reading on my part, I'm sorry to say. My fragile reputation would be enhanced immeasurably by such a skill. No, I must confess to prior knowledge.

"During the Ripper investigation there were certain pieces of information that it was thought desirable to keep from the public. In this way the police could separate genuine information the public provided from the imaginings of the many cranks—and worse—who emerge at such times and cause Lestrade and his friends to pursue false and pointless trails.

"There were two incidental things that were noted at each of the proven murders. A man was heard to whistle *Auprès de Ma Blonde*— sometimes accompanied by a laugh—and there was the sound of a metal door being closed. Since so many other components of a Ripper crime seemed to be in place, it was a reasonable assumption that this might follow.

"Watson, I very much fear that we are at the beginning of a new and even more terrible phase. This man has not merely sneaked back to his home land. He seems determined to—what was that phrase in Marlowe's *Tamburlaine?*—'ride in triumph through Persepolis.' Take a look at this . . ."

And with that he threw a folded copy of the morning's *Times* into my lap.

"As you know, I rarely read anything but the criminal news and that chorus of groans, cries and bleatings that passes today for the agony columns. However, this morning there is one rather chilling message to be found there . . ."

I saw that he had marked one particular item with a slash of his pencil. It read . . .

A FALLEN WOMAN

And beneath it . . .

"Who can find a virtuous woman?"
(Proverbs – 31:10)

I was still trying to make head or tail of it, when Holmes interrupted my train of thought.

"So what do you deduce from that, my dear Watson?"

"Lady Hatton . . . pushed down area steps . . . 'fallen woman'?"

"Excellent, Watson! I think we can ignore 'virtuous woman'—the writer is speaking metaphorically there. But surely you detect something else . . . ?"

Seeing that I was at a loss, he continued . . .

"To place an advertisement in this morning's paper, whoever arranged it did so *before* the murder. He is taunting us. Here I am—catch me if you can. But the question is—*who* is he? Who is he *now?*"

We sat there in silence for a moment, each of us lost in our own thoughts. For my own part I was remembering the chill that had descended during those few horrendous months nearly seven years ago. Although the Ripper had confined himself to the East End of London, no woman had felt truly safe. This new horror would simply reawaken that sleeping fear and to find that he was now abroad in the heart of the city . . .

My reverie was interrupted by a tap on the door and Mrs. Hudson entered to clear the breakfast things and deliver the morning's post.

Holmes snatched at the larger pile that bore his name and began discarding most of the letters, where they joined the mess of crumpled papers around his feet. Mrs. Hudson and I exchanged a sympathetic glance. When he was in this mood, there was no point in arguing.

"Hm—a letter here from a coal merchant in Walsall convinced that his neighbours are Nihilists, because he has seen them smoking Russian cigarettes. Will I please investigate? Really! I must admit that there is a charming unpredictability about my post bag most mornings but spies in the coal shed . . . ! Hello—what's this? A social summons, unless I am very much mistaken."

From where I was sitting I could see that the paper he had unfolded from the envelope was some sort of playbill. He examined it from every angle, as was his wont with anything that caught his interest.

"Ah, our mystery correspondent has a message for us on the back." And he read aloud—" '*Gentlemen—Your seats await you for this evening's performance. For once the piece does not have to have an unhappy ending!*' "

"And what piece might that be?" I asked.

"*La Traviata*. Verdi at his full-blown romantic best," Holmes replied, holding up the paper, so that I could see the front display. "Frankly, if it had been a Wagner night . . . Verdi is a little sweet for my tooth . . ."

He stopped in mid-sentence and then held the sheet up to the morning light streaming through the window. Then across his face passed one of the strangest expressions I have ever seen there. Disbelief followed by—was it excitement?— before it set into the blank Red Indian stare that he liked to affect when he was experiencing conflicting emotions.

"Is everything all right, Holmes?"

"Do you know, old fellow, I'm not at all sure," was the strange reply. Then—"Perhaps I am being unduly hard on the good Giuseppe. A little old-fashioned sentiment might be good for my soul. If you have no other plans, I suggest we resume our interrupted supper and stroll across to Covent Garden. We are not presented with so many gift horses that we can afford to look them in the mouth."

And with that he tucked the folded playbill carefully into his dressing-gown pocket.

I had a number of errands to attend to which kept me occupied for much of the day and, as soon as he had dressed, Holmes also left the house—I presumed to confer with Lestrade and his colleagues on the events of the previous evening.

It was early evening, therefore, before I saw my friend again and we barely had sufficient time to change and pile into a hansom on our way to Simpson's.

As we bowled through the West End, it was clear what the burning topic of the hour was. All the newsboys had placards that read—

LEADING SOCIETY WOMAN
SLASHED!

. . . and—

SON OF RIPPER STRIKES AGAIN?

I turned to say something about it to my companion, only to find his brows set in that single hard line that betokened both concentration and frustration.

"No, Watson, this isn't a repetition of that *annus horribilis* 1888, I'd be prepared to bet on it. This is simply meant to *look* like it. It's the old conjuror's trick of *légerdemain*—making us all look in one direction while something is happening in another. And the quotation from the Bible . . . These are deep waters, Watson—perhaps the deepest we have ever encountered."

An excellent dinner did much to revive our spirits and we emerged on a cold but bright January evening before setting off on the short walk to the Opera House.

The Strand was its usual bustling self with the crowds passing in and out of the gaslights, forming a theatre all their own. How many personal tragedies and triumphs were crossing our path every moment in this great city, if only we knew the plots?

Glancing at my companion, I could not help but reflect on the transformation evening clothes wrought in him. Although he stood just over six feet, that lean frame of his gave an impression of even greater height and the chiselled, aquiline face—now seen in profile—put me in mind of no one so much as Henry Irving, whose beloved Lyceum Theatre we were now passing, having decided to take a short detour in view of the fine evening. As I have often had cause to remark in my "little narratives," the stage lost an actor of stature when Sherlock Holmes chose to deal instead with the dramas of daily life.

The Royal Opera House always presents a glittering spectacle itself, regardless of what is playing there. If I were to be perfectly honest, I would have to admit that on more than one occasion in the past I have found the show before the show, so to speak, to be the more interesting.

Tonight's offering, however, was one of my favourites and I looked forward to what was to come.

We arrived with a few minutes to spare and, as we promenaded through the foyer, I noticed a number of people reacting to my friend's presence in a variety of ways.

Some would greet him formally and effusively; others would wait until he had passed and nudge one another, nodding in his direction. One or two would look positively apprehensive, avoid his gaze and seek to lose themselves in the convenient crowd.

One particular gentleman, who was clearly lording it loudly over a party of elegantly-attired guests, stopped in mid speech and lost his colour entirely, much to the surprise—and, I suspect, relief—of his companions. Holmes merely raised his hat to the group politely and moved on, murmuring to me out of the side of his mouth—"Surely you recognise X, the Member of Parliament in that curious business involving the trained cormorant and the lighthouse, Watson? I do believe the world may be ready for your telling of that particular tale. What's more, I believe the gentleman in question believes so, too."

The *comédie humaine* of which we were plainly a part distracted me for the moment from the surprising circumstances of our arrival. For when

40

we presented ourselves at the box office, we were immediately presented with two excellent seats that had been reserved in our names. There was absolutely no indication of our mysterious benefactor. The seats, when we came to take them, were in the most advantageous part of the stalls.

As we settled in our seats, I saw Holmes open his programme and a moment later I did the same. A small piece of paper that had been tucked inside it fluttered to the ground at my feet. Retrieving it, I glanced at it casually and then, I swear, when I saw what was printed there, my jaw dropped. It's a phrase we writers often resort to but I had never really considered its literal meaning until now.

I turned to look at Holmes and needed no clairvoyant to tell that he, too, had read those same words—

The management regrets that Madame —— is indisposed. At this evening's performance of La Traviata, the part of Violetta will be sung by Miss Irene Adler

For a moment the great auditorium and its sea of faces seemed a blur.

Irene Adler. For Holmes she had always been *the* woman. How often had I heard him say that during his whole career to date he had been beaten by only three men and one woman—and that woman was Irene Adler.

The case had involved the King of Bohemia and a highly inconvenient photograph of the two of them together. Holmes had seemed poised to retrieve it and bring the case to his usual tidy conclusion but the adventuress had outsmarted him. At the last moment she had suddenly married—what was the lawyer fellow's name? Norton. Godfrey Norton—and left the country but not before trumping Holmes, the master of disguise, at his own game.

When it was opened, the cupboard that supposedly held the incriminating picture turned out to be as bare as the one in the nursery rhyme. Certainly, what it contained was a photograph but it was a solo portrait of the elusive Miss Adler herself and a teasing note addressed to Holmes. Strangely, the souvenir of *"the* woman" (as he always referred to her thereafter) seemed to satisfy him as much as any conventional fee. I happened to know that he kept it in a drawer in his room and on more than one occasion I had caught a glimpse of him looking at it when he thought himself unobserved.

I tried to remember what I knew of the lady from the entry in Holmes's index. Born in New Jersey in 1858. That would make her—what? Thirty-seven. A former diva with the Imperial Opera of Warsaw . . . played at La Scala in Milan and many of the other leading houses. Retired in mid-career, presumably to take up more lucrative pursuits. Since the affair of "A Scandal in Bohemia"—as I had entitled my account in the *Strand Magazine*—in 1888, seven long years ago, the lady had vanished from our ken . . . There had been rumours that she had died under mysterious circumstances.

And now . . .

All of this passed through my mind in a flash as I looked at my old friend. . . .

I'm quite prepared to admit that the fault is largely mine but I do find that the plots of some of these modern operas strain one's belief—and, frankly, if one understood a word they were singing, it would only make matters worse. I'd seen this particular piece more than once and become inured to the sight of a lady who is supposed to be genteelly dying of consumption being played by a buxom creature singing at the top of her voice.

Imagine my surprise, then, when Irene Adler appeared as Violetta. When she and Holmes crossed swords and paths during that business with the King of Bohemia, I never actually met the woman face to face—merely saw her in the distance. I have to say that in no way did the photograph do her justice. I remembered an appealing heart-shaped face and a pair of haunting eyes but what I was not prepared for was the animation she possessed. When she was on stage one could not look away.

She *was* Violetta—capricious, flirtatious yet vulnerable . . . and clearly doomed. And when she sang her great first act aria . . .

E strano . . . Ah! Forse è lui . . .

. . . that huge house was silent for what seemed like an age when she had finished before it erupted into an ovation such as I have heard only for the proven legends.

There she stood, accepting the acclaim, a woman in the full bloom of her confidence and beauty. What had happened to her in the intervening years, I wondered? Her sudden departure from London to avoid the persecution of her former lover, the pompous Bohemian (for him I *had* met)—or even the professional attention of the gentleman sitting next to me— had involved no criminal act. She was perfectly entitled to be back on British soil, if she so chose. But what had happened to Norton, the lawyer she had married? Since the speculation without benefit of facts was quite pointless, I settled back in my seat and let Verdi's melodies wash over me and slowly but surely raise my spirits. How very different, I reflected, from last evening.

In my peripheral vision—for I did not wish to make my scrutiny obvious to Holmes—I could see that my friend was every bit as transported as I. The tension I had observed when the curtain rose had disappeared and I could see those long, thin fingers start to wave in time to the music—a sure sign that he had let the barriers drop. I would have given a good deal to know what thoughts were revolving in *his* mind.

As the curtain fell for the interval, I turned in his direction.

"Well, Holmes, what a turn up . . ."—only to find that he was speaking to a young Opera House page who had just handed him a folded note.

"Excuse me, Watson. A summons from the Corridors of Power." And he was gone. I could not help but sense that he was quite glad of the temporary reprieve from my questioning, as I was left to do what he so often advised—namely to possess my soul in patience.

I have often noticed in public gatherings of this kind that some sort of cosmic field force operates around Holmes. People are aware of his presence and, when he removes himself from the scene for some reason, one can sense they feel a void. This has a rather interesting side effect, in that they are inclined to totally overlook my being there, as their eyes follow him. Many a time I have gleaned valuable information in my role of invisible observer.

On this occasion I was overcome with a strong sense of someone focusing intently not on Holmes but on his empty seat. I am never quite sure why one is made so physically aware of another person's psychic energy being deployed in this way but it is an undoubted phenomenon and on this occasion I was in no doubt as to its origin.

Raising and polishing the spectacles I have recently taken to wearing—purely to read small print in a dimly-lit environment, you understand—I was able to employ their lens as a rudimentary mirror.

Sitting a few rows behind us was a most extraordinary figure. Even seated, he was undoubtedly a tall and imposing man, shrouded in a black opera cloak. This in itself I found mildly surprising, since the hall was perfectly well heated. He wore a moustache and full beard which completely covered the lower part of his face. Unfortunately, it also drew attention to his mouth, which was particularly thin, a virtual slit, with lips as crimson as any woman's. His hair was wild, long and flowing down to his shoulders. In fact, he reminded me of nothing so much as a painting of some Old Testament prophet suddenly transported to the nineteenth century.

But what really rivetted my attention were his eyes. I could not be sure without turning in my seat—which would have defeated the purpose of the exercise entirely—but I could have sworn the pupils were of a deep purple, verging on black. I had never seen such a gaze. It seemed to bore though everything in its path.

The whole experience was beginning to make me physically uncomfortable and I was more than curious to know the identity of this man who would have seemed more at home on the other side of the footlights. It was at this point that Holmes slipped back in to the seat next to me.

"Signor Verdi should write a new opera and call it *Jupiter Descending*—or whatever the Italian equivalent happens to be. You will never guess, Watson, who I have just been talking to?"

"Holmes, I have had quite enough surprises for one day," I replied. "I am in no mood for guessing games. Who?"

"My brother Mycroft. As I'm sure I have often told you, Mycroft's life runs on rails. Whitehall to the Diogenes Club to his apartments opposite and back to Whitehall. For him to undertake the additional half mile or so to Covent Garden is like a planet leaving its preordained orbit—yet here he is. Or, rather, *there* he is . . ."

And he indicated one of the boxes, where several eminent-looking folk, drooping under the weight of their insignia, were chatting in a desultory fashion. Standing slightly to one side of them and obviously in official attendance was the massive figure of Mycroft Holmes, Sherlock's elder brother.

Mycroft remained an enigma to me. I had met him only once face to face, during the affair of "The Greek Interpreter" some seven years or so earlier. No, in fact, come to think of it, that is not quite true. A heavily muffled and silent Mycroft had been the "coachman" who drove me to Victoria to meet Holmes, as we started our mad European dash to avoid Moriarty—that trip, which led to the disaster at Reichenbach in May of 1891. And it was Mycroft, I later learned, who maintained Holmes's estate during the three years of the "Great Hiatus."

I knew little about him to this day. A creature of habit, certainly. Highly placed in government circles, undoubtedly. According to Holmes, his brother, to all intents and purposes, frequently *was* the government. Few matters of con-sequence, it seemed, were decided without Mycroft's *imprimatur*.

And there he stood just above and to one side of us, like a corpulent statue—as different in appearance from that lean "greyhound in the slips," his younger brother, as it was possible to imagine. Until one looked at the eyes. They were a peculiarly light gray in colour and seemed to have at all times that faraway, introspective look which I had only ever observed in my friend when he was exerting his full powers.

As I was contemplating that living graven image, I heard Holmes murmur—"As you say, Watson—curiouser and curiouser. Mycroft insists on taking us for dinner tomorrow night but not to his benighted Diogenes Club. The

Café Royal, no less, where we have at least a chance of something adequate to eat. Something is most definitely afoot and, although he was not prepared to discuss it until tomorrow, I don't think we have far to seek to discern his agenda, eh?"

As if on cue, the house lights dimmed and we returned to the players in the other drama that was taking place on the stage.

In those two final acts Irene Adler held that audience in her elegant little hand. From what little I had heard of her previous career, I would have expected a run-of-the-mill soprano with the vocal demands of Violetta well beyond her range. Perhaps the voice had matured with age but, in any case, I was completely in error. The woman was simply superb. When Violetta dies, I found myself clearing my throat and dabbing at my eyes and I could deduce from the noises around me that I was not alone.

Addio del passato bel sogno ridenti
Le rose del volto già sono pallenti . . .
Delia traviata . . . sorridi . . . al desio.
A lei, deh persona, tu accoglia, o Dio!
Ah! Tutto fini,
Or tutto fini.

The curtain fell to a tumult of applause, then rose and fell more times than I could count.

Finally, Irene Adler was left alone in the centre of the stage, clutching her bouquets, as the whole house rose to her. I sensed Holmes fidgeting next to me, then felt him relax as a page dashed on stage with one final garland—a magnificent arrangement of white roses. Miss Adler accepted with a charming smile for the boy and—was it my imagination?—seemed to look in our direction.

The curtain fell for the last time and we were back in the real world, a world buzzing with speculation about this wonderful "new" talent. Only Holmes was silent, as we gathered our things together, preparatory to leaving.

It suddenly occurred to me to draw Holmes's attention to the Prophet who had rivetted my attention earlier. Such an unusual fellow must surely be known to the man who knew everything? But when I turned to point him out, the seat he had been occupying was already empty and the thought soon became submerged by the more pressing question of the hour. What was the meaning of Irene Adler's dramatic return to London after so long? And how would it affect Sherlock Holmes?

In the cab I tried several times in my tactful way to broach the subject but each time Holmes managed to glide on to another tack. Finally, he turned and caught my eye for the first time since the *erratum* slip had fallen out of the programme.

"My dear old friend," he said, "I am perfectly

prepared to discuss shoes and ships and sealing wax or cabbages and kings. I will even, if you so wish, debate with you miracle plays, medieval pottery or the Buddhism of Ceylon. Beyond that I am not prepared to go."

Since I had no pressing interest in any of the above, the rest of the journey back to Baker Street passed uneventfully, not to say silently.

Once we had closed the door behind us, Holmes went straight to his room with a polite but firm "Goodnight." I myself, though, was so enervated by what I had just experienced that I determined to have a nightcap before turning in. As I settled myself in my chair, I found I was about to sit on a folded piece of paper.

Picking it up and smoothing out the creases, I saw that it was the handbill for the performance we had just seen. Presumably Holmes had dropped it there on his way to bed.

It was then that I noticed something about it that had escaped me earlier. Holding it up to the gas jet confirmed it. Where the title LA TRAVIATA was printed someone had made a circle of pinpricks that contained two of the letters . . .

IA

One did not need to be Sherlock Holmes to deduce what those letters stood for . . .

CHAPTER FOUR

As I get older I find that, if I retire with my mind in a turmoil, I invariably dream and that night was no exception. I lay there, my mind teeming with the thoughts and impressions of the last two days and then, suddenly, I was in a fairground that seemed to go on for ever.

Except for me, everyone was walking through it in slow motion and I noticed that there was no joy on any of their faces. *How strange,* I found myself thinking, *why do they call this a* fun *fair? They should call it a* fright *fair.* For some reason this thought amused me immoderately and I began to laugh but for some reason I could not hear a sound above the noise of the hurdy-gurdy and the shouts of the barkers.

I passed a coconut shy where Lestrade in bowler hat and raincoat was throwing an endless series of wooden balls at the coconuts. On looking closer, though, I could see that each coconut was the head of the unfortunate McLinsky, who had his eyes screwed up in anticipation of being hit. Lestrade was saying to me—"Come on, Doctor, it's not difficult. We're trained to do this sort of thing at the Yard."

Then I was in a Hall of Mirrors, which was quite deserted except for myself and at the far end Sherlock and Mycroft Holmes, who were deep in conversation, though, again, I could not hear a word. As they moved around, the mirrors distorted their images so that the tall slender figure of Holmes would turn into the corpulent one of Mycroft, then back again. The spectacle was so disquieting that I heard myself crying— "I do wish you two would make your minds up!" At which the two images became one and immediately vanished.

Now I was on a carousel and, as I looked around, I could see that, again, I was the only customer. Round and round went the gaily-painted horses, up and down on their ornate and twisted poles. I strained to hear the music that was playing and realised that it was Violetta's final aria from *La Traviata*. "Well, this is all wrong," I thought to myself. "Verdi wouldn't approve of this at all."

Nonetheless, the rhythm was certainly relaxing me and I looked down at the horse on which I was riding. It was a magnificent creature, far more impressive than any I had ridden on as a boy. I found I had my hands firmly wrapped around its mane, which was long and blond and coarse to the touch.

This is really quite fun, I thought and impulsively gave the horse's flanks a kick with my heels and pulled on the mane to encourage my trusty steed to greater efforts.

Again, everything seemed to decelerate and the music became suddenly discordant, like a gramophone winding down. But the truly horrible thing was that the horse's head came away in my hands and turned to face me. Except that it wasn't a *horse's* head at all any longer—but the head of a man with long blond hair and dead blue-black eyes. His throat had been cut and the blood was running down my arms . . .

I cried out and tried to throw it from me but the hair was tangled around my wrists. And then I heard a woman's voice say . . .

"Oh, Doctor, now look what you've done. You've spilled your tea all over the sheets!"

And there was the face of Mrs. Hudson looking down at me. It was then that I realised that my hands were caught up in the sodden bed sheets.

"I was just leaning over you to put your tea on the bedside table when you sat bolt upright and knocked it out of my hands. Never mind, Doctor, it was my day for changing the sheets anyway. Here's your dressing-gown and I'll soon fetch another cup. I know you like to start your day with one."

Then over her shoulder, as she reached the door . . .

"Mr. Holmes has been up for ages, making a terrible smell—what with those chemicals of his *and* that awful tobacco . . ."

I was in that half state between waking and dreaming, when your mind tells you that the thing that's still disturbing you was all in your mind but yet it still seems more real than the world you're now once again fighting to inhabit.

I've often thought some clever person should write about the meaning of dreams—perhaps that Viennese fellow, Freud that Holmes has been talking about so much lately. Usually, if you take the trouble, you can relate what you've dreamed about to things that have been happening around you but sometimes I get the feeling that one is anticipating what you feel or fear *may* happen.

And then, for a split second, I found myself thinking about the man who had been sitting a few rows behind us at the opera. Something about the eyes. And then it was gone.

Some time later, having enjoyed an unspilt cup of tea and a leisurely toilet, I descended to the sitting room in much improved spirits to find that Mrs. Hudson had not exaggerated. The room was a fug. Someone less experienced than myself in the ways of my friend and associate might easily have called for the services of the Fire Brigade.

Nonetheless, as I grew accustomed to the haze, I could see that Holmes, too, had recovered his usual *sang-froid*. His battered old briar pipe clutched between his teeth, he was bent over the corner table that held his scientific paraphernalia, doing something which clearly required intense concentration.

"Morning, Holmes," I said cheerfully. On these occasions one never knows whether or not to expect a reply. To my surprise I received a positively euphoric one.

"An *excellent* morning, old fellow. Excellent. Now, come over here. There is something I particularly wish to show you."

I did as he asked, to find him holding up a test tube full of a clear liquid. Inside, floating in the solution was what looked like a single human hair—a long blond hair.

"You will remember the other night, Watson . . ."

"Ah, yes, I meant to ask you about that, Holmes. I had supposed that the lady must have brushed against one of her colleagues earlier in the evening?"

"She was obviously in contact with *someone* but I fancy it was not one of the Daughters of Eve. This hair comes from a man's head—and it was recently dyed."

"Good heavens, Holmes!"

"Cuvier, thou shouldst be living at this hour! You have heard me speak of the work of Georges Cuvier, Watson, the late and distinguished French naturalist?"

I nodded vaguely. It did not do to interrupt him when he was in full flow.

"Cuvier could take a single bone and describe to you the whole animal. We owe the art of reconstructing the corpse of a victim almost entirely to him. I am merely, in my humble way, seeking to develop his line of thinking. Beyond the fact that this hair comes from the head of a healthy male approximately six feet in height and in a good state of health, I can tell nothing. But one day, Watson, one day we shall be able to take a hair or a fingernail or even a piece of skin tissue—a single drop of blood even—and get to know the host as if they were an old friend. Imagine!"

"Rather a creepy feeling, Holmes, if you don't mind my saying so. Bits of dead skin turning themselves into whole bodies. I'm not sure I really want to know . . ."

My reaction—predictable as I'm sure it was—seemed to amuse him enough to allow me time to eat my breakfast and for him to pack away his toys.

"Nonetheless, old fellow," he said, as we sat over our after-breakfast pipes, "the fact remains that Lady Hatton *was* in contact with a man whose appearance is, to say the least, unconventional for this day and age and it is more than possible that the man killed her."

"But what man would wear his hair that long, unless he was an actor? And surely he wouldn't walk around the streets like that?"

"A valid point, Watson. Unless, of course, he is playing a public role that calls for it . . ."

And then I remembered the man from the opera . . . the man in my dream. But as I was about to say something, supposing I could have put it into words, we heard the front door bell give its familiar clang.

Holmes sat bolt upright in his chair, a thing I have never seen him do before. Usually he likes to play a little game of trying to guess what kind of person our visitor will be and he is particularly good when it comes to our female "guests."

An aggressive ring is a woman bent on retribution; a hesitant peal an *affaire du coeur*— and so on. But, clearly, this was different and his attention was already engaged. And then the penny dropped.

"But, Holmes, how can you be sure?"

"Believe me, Watson, I am absolutely sure."

There was an expression on his face such as I had seen only once before and that the previous evening. Had I not known better, I should have guessed that it owed something to his beloved seven per cent solution, from which I think I had almost succeeded in weaning him. He was like a small boy summoned to the headmaster's study and not sure whether he is to hear good news or ill.

There was a tap at the door and Mrs. Hudson's face appeared around it.

"A Mrs. Norton to see you, Mr. Holmes." And then—"Oh, my goodness, and the breakfast things still on the table! What *will* she think?"

Bless that dear woman. What with her nonstop apologies and the bustling around with trays and crockery, she provided covering fire, so to speak, and I had a distinct feeling that her performance was quite deliberate.

In any event, by the time she had withdrawn, Irene Adler was in the room and arranging herself in the visitors' basket chair facing Holmes.

And now I saw *the* woman clearly for the first time. Not frozen in the artificial pose of a photographer's flash. Not painted in broad strokes to project across a theatre's footlights.

She was not, perhaps, a true beauty in the classical sense of a Lillie Langtry but she was something infinitely more. She was a life force. Strictly speaking, perhaps the mouth was a little too wide, the brow a little too broad but none of that mattered. The face was alive with intelligence and humour. I could detect a few small lines at the corners of her fine blue eyes but they were the only signs of the passing years and, frankly, they merely added character and spoke of an amused tolerance of life's absurdities.

I recalled what Holmes had reported when he had first returned from observing her in her home. "She has turned all the men's heads down in that part," he said. "She is the daintiest thing under a bonnet on this planet," was the verdict of the local male population. And it had seemed to me then—as it seemed to me now—that that verdict was not restricted to one locality.

Miss Adler—Mrs. Norton—was neatly but not ostentatiously dressed. There was no sign of the flaunting *diva* about her. Nonetheless, the simple morning gown suggested that she retained the superb figure I had observed all those years ago. It took me no time at all to understand why my friend should determine that this woman was *the* woman . . .

Having completed the tasks that every woman feels the need to complete before she is settled, Miss Adler raised her eyes and looked at Holmes directly for the first time. I felt I was watching some medieval challenge between two champions.

"Well, Mr. Sherlock Holmes . . . ?"

"Well, Miss Adler . . . ?"

"You are wondering why I have sought you out?"

"Holmes," I interrupted, "I think I should . . ." and began to rise from my chair.

"No, old fellow." Holmes seized my wrist in a firm grip. "I had rather you stayed. I'm sure Miss Adler won't object?"

"Indeed, not, Doctor. I have been reading your chronicles during my—sabbatical, and I know very well that without Doctor Watson there *is* no

Sherlock Holmes. I am delighted to meet you at last."

The eyes were turned fully in my direction and immediately the secret of her charm was apparent to me. This woman had the power to make the object of her attention—however temporary—feel that they were the only person in the universe in whom she had the slightest interest. But whereas Medusa had turned men to stone, this experience was infinitely more enervating. I considered myself duly enslaved.

Holmes's voice brought me back to reality.

"Miss Adler, you both see *and* observe. I am extremely curious to know to what the good Doctor and I owe this reappearance. The last time we met, if I recall correctly, you were slouching past our door dressed as a young man? I much prefer your present persona . . ."

At which Irene Adler laughed—a genuine, full-throated laugh. And suddenly the tension in the room evaporated and the three of us were laughing like so many school children. What Mrs. Hudson must have made of it I have no idea but I had a shrewd suspicion that she was busying herself not too far away from the door.

Miss Adler wiped her eye with the tiniest handkerchief I have ever seen and leaned forward in her chair.

"Oh, Sherlock Holmes," she said. Her eyes were still moist and I somehow felt that the tears were from relief as much as laughter.

"I may call you Sherlock, may I not? This is old acquaintance in a way and I for one have certainly not forgot . . ."

Holmes returned her gaze—and once more I felt *de trop*. Laughter was not something in which he often indulged and he seemed loth to give it up. However, there was something in the lady's expression to which he responded in kind.

"Only if I may exchange 'Miss Adler' for— 'Irene' . . ."

At that moment I knew we had all crossed a personal Rubicon.

And then Irene told us the story of the years between . . .

"I need hardly remind you of my hasty departure in May of 1888 . . ."

"Indeed not," said Holmes, "the date of ignominy is engraved on both our hearts, eh, Watson?"

"You are the one woman who has ever defeated the world's greatest consulting detective, madam, and I have often sworn that if I have to listen to the story one more time . . ."

"Oh, you do not know how often I have wanted to correct you both on that," Irene exclaimed. "When I read your account in—'A Scandal in Bohemia,' I believe you called it?—I almost wrote to you but I didn't think I had the right . . .

"That whole business with the late—and by

me, at least, unlamented—King of Bohemia was a farce from beginning to end. Yes, I had a photograph of the two of us, which, I suppose, could be called a little embarrassing to a man who is preparing to marry a prudish stick insect of a princess. Frankly, they deserved one another for, I must tell you, that the gentleman from Bohemia was one of the most boring, boastful, self-obsessed men it has been my misfortune to meet . . ."

"But the photograph?" I heard myself say and then wished I could have bitten back the words.

"I had no intention of sending that to her or anyone else, John . . ." *John!*

"I simply wanted to make that stupid man suffer a little. We women occasionally indulge ourselves in these childish impulses, as I'm sure you gentlemen well know . . ."

"Ah, yes," I nodded knowingly. I turned to Holmes for corroboration but he might as well have been carved from granite.

". . . and, by the sounds of it, I succeeded. And by the way, my spies tell me the marriage was a disaster!"

"And Mr. Norton?" We authors constantly need to verify our material.

"Ah, Godfrey?" And the animation left her face. "Godfrey Norton is one of the less admirable episodes of my life, I'm afraid. Godfrey loved me. I liked him well enough. And when the time came that I felt I must flee from London, well . . . I suppose I used him. Oh, I told myself I felt as much for him as I could for anyone and that—as they say in the cheap novels—my love for him would grow, once we were free of this place . . ."

"But I take it the novels were misinformed?" Holmes spoke for the first time.

She nodded sadly. "You have no idea how much I wished for a happy ending. But instead . . ." She fixed her eyes on the cluttered shelves behind his head. "Godfrey suffered from consumption. We travelled a great deal and, I suppose, that was not too wise in his condition. Within a year he was dead and I was alone. My only consolation was that he never really knew how I felt. To the day he died he felt that we were the ideal couple.

"But none of this explains why I did what I did . . ."

Holmes fixed her with that intense stare of his.

"Of that I have no doubt. But what did?"

"Fear. Pure blind fear. I feared for my life!"

"But my dear girl, how . . ." I could not help myself. I could see that Irene was gripping her handkerchief tightly. Whatever she was about to relate was still able to cause her great distress.

"It had been happening for some weeks before you and I—met . . ." Now Holmes was the sole object of her story.

"As I went to and fro I was conscious of being followed but I could never quite see the person who was doing the following. It was as though they were playing a game with me. I was meant to know. At first I thought the King was behind it and, as you know, he did have professional burglars search my little house for that ridiculous photograph. In vain, I might add . . ." She gave a small smile of satisfaction.

"But this was something different, something strangely disturbing. Someone, for some unknown reason, was—how can I put it?—stalking me. And then the flowers started to arrive. Always white roses. Oh, thank you for last night. They meant a great deal to me . . ."

Holmes was as close to blushing as I have ever seen him. He busied himself filling one of his less disreputable pipes. We men have our own ways of deflecting awkward attention.

"They would be left on the doorstep, in my dressing room, at the occasional concert halls where I performed. Never a message. Nothing to indicate who the sender was. But somehow a message was conveyed. Somehow the atmosphere seemed to grow more intense as the weeks went by, as if I were not doing something that was expected of me.

"And then one morning something snapped in me. I opened my front door and there were the flowers. I lost my temper and stood on the doorstep, screaming like a fishwife—'This has to stop! Whoever you are, you must be out of

65

your mind. For God's sake, leave me alone!'

"Whoever it was must have been in earshot, for next morning the flowers were there again but—here is the thing that terrified me—they were cut into pieces . . . and sprinkled with what looked like *blood!* As I bent to look at them, I heard someone nearby start to whistle. It was a silly little nursery rhyme sort of tune . . ."

Those magnificent eyes opened wide. "Yes, that's it. But how did you guess?"

Holmes had just whistled the first six notes of *Auprès de Ma Blonde*.

"In a moment. Pray continue, omitting no detail, however trivial."

"And every day thereafter, the same thing happened. Sometimes at the house, sometimes at places no one could have anticipated that I would be. Always the flowers, the whistling, occasionally a man's mocking laugh and, once or twice—now, you will probably put this down to a foolish woman's imaginings . . ."

"A metallic sound, as of a heavy door being closed?"

"You *are* the devil they say you are. How can you possibly know these things?"

"It is my business to know things other people do not."

"I swear to you, gentlemen, there was evil abroad. I could feel it. And, foolishly, I had somehow crossed this evil. I truly felt that my life

66

was in danger. And so, the rest you know. I was a coward for all my bravura—I admit it. A coward to panic and a coward to use another to help me escape. Only one thing happened subsequently to make me feel that perhaps I had not been so foolish after all . . ."

"And that was . . . ?"

"When all those poor women started to be butchered two or three months later. There *was* evil abroad and I knew I had felt its wings beating over me. But then, as the years went by, and my travels took me thither and yon, the memory began to fade . . ."

"We heard you were dead, though," I inter-jected.

"Irene Adler *was* dead," she answered quietly. "Irene Norton remained my name until I returned a few weeks ago. I kept no contacts with old friends and then, when poor Godfrey died, those few people who still cared must have confused his death with mine and so the rumour began. But, as you can see, the rumours of my death have been greatly exaggerated." And with some effort the actress in her summoned back the smile.

"One more thing and my story is over—but it is this that brings me back into your life, Sherlock Holmes . . . and, if I am honest, a woman's curiosity to see how the years have used you.

"My work is the one thing that has kept me sane

67

these past years. Under a number of different pseudonyms I have performed all over Europe and when the offer came from Covent Garden to understudy some of the leading roles this season, I felt that Fate was taking a hand. It was telling me that it was time to return, that all was well once again. And so back I came . . . and what a horrible mistake I have made!"

"But why do you say that?" I asked. "You had a triumph last night as Violetta. Why, I said to Holmes . . ."

"But you see, that has only made things worse," she cried, almost rising from her seat. "When I returned to my dressing room, happier than I can remember being in my life . . ."—she darted a glance at Holmes—"there were the flowers again.

". . . and the blood! And then that infernal laughter. Sherlock—it is starting all over again! What am I to do?"

And then, to my eternal surprise, two things happened.

Holmes leaned forward and took Irene Adler's hand in both of his. He then proceeded to give her an account—admittedly edited and abbreviated—of the Jack the Ripper story. Strangely, instead of disturbing her further, it seemed to calm her.

"Well," she said when he had finished, giving us both a tremulous smile, "at least now I know that it is not I who am going mad. But what does it all mean—and why me?"

Holmes released her hand a little self-consciously and, picking up his pipe again, sat back in his chair, puffing smoke at the ceiling as he gathered his thoughts.

"Our killer—whoever he is . . ."—for, naturally, he had not revealed the name—"is a man who has lived for years on the edge of a mental abyss.

"He was *of* society—in fact, there are indications that he was highly placed in that society . . ."

How much, I wondered, was Holmes now deducing and how much was prior knowledge speaking?

". . . but he never felt part of it. His sense of inadequacy was perhaps sexual in part but by far the greater part was social. No one understood him and, if they did, they would surely despise him. Every day must have been an increasing torment to him, as he tried to act a part, to find a key to his personal conundrum. And then he met you . . ."

"But I did nothing!" The flicker of a small muscle at the angle of that sculpted jaw was the only sign of the tension Irene Adler was clearly feeling.

"Let me re-phrase that—when he realised that you existed. Irrationally, I suspect he saw you as the embodiment of his answer. It would not be the first time that one person has sought to find a part of themselves in someone else, projected their hopes and fears on someone else . . ."

There was a moment's silence and I kept my eyes averted, for I knew that, however fleetingly, they must be looking at one another.

Holmes continued.

"But, believe me, there is nothing with which you should reproach yourself. The railway train hits the person who happens to cross its path. It is not the fault of the person. It is not necessarily the fault of the train, even though this train was picking up speed and was destined to leave its tracks. But that person is identified ever after as the designated victim. And somehow that train is now back on the track."

"This talk about trains is all very well, Holmes, but what is the woman to do now?"

Holmes ignored my question but he rose and began pacing the room, a sure sign that he was weighing alternatives. Those heavy brows were drawn into a single black line and his eyes were on infinity.

"I have no doubt you are in great danger. What are your further commitments at the Opera?"

"I play Senta this evening in *The Flying Dutchman* and then nothing until a new production in two weeks . . ."

"By which time—for good or ill—this ill-starred business will have been brought to a conclusion, I trust.

"Pray be careful for the remainder of the day. Stay where there are crowds. Where are you lodging?"

Irene mentioned a modest hotel just behind the Strand.

"Pack your things and take them with you to the theatre. Doctor Watson and I will come there and collect you at the end of the performance and take you to a boarding house run by a friend of Mrs. Hudson's. The woman is most discreet and the accommodations clean and comfortable. We have had occasion to make use of her services more than once in the past. You will be safe there for the next few days."

And then Irene Adler smiled and stood. For a moment I was transported back to that evening long ago when I saw that splendid figure silhouetted outside the front door of her home at Briony Lodge. It took little imagination to see how a man might believe that she could change his universe.

Without saying a word, she crossed the room towards us. Instead of shaking Holmes's hand, she simply laid hers very gently on his arm. Turning only slightly, she placed her other hand on mine and for an instant we were all linked in some sort of bond.

The next thing I knew she was at the door and

I was aware that this was an actress making an exit.

"As Violetta might say—'A *bientôt*, gentlemen!' "

And then we were alone.

CHAPTER FIVE

"Thank you, gentlemen, for sparing me the time. Knowing that my brother has his reservations about dining at my club, I have thought it best to arrange a little snack here at the Café Royal, a venue that apparently does meet with his approval."

Mycroft Holmes waved his arm in an expansive manner to indicate the laden table in the *salon privé* to which a deferential *maître d'* had led us. The slightly overwrought décor of the place has always been a little excessive for my own taste but Holmes seemed to like it and it was certainly to be preferred to the spartan appointments of the Diogenes Club, that "club for the unclubable."

"I fear, Mycroft, that for once you are being economical with the truth. The food at the Diogenes is perfectly adequate—as long as one does not mind dining in a crypt. But I must admit that this does look somewhat superior . . ."

We were all relaxed over a whisky and water, nobody more so than Mycroft himself. That huge body filled the largest available chair to overflowing, yet "fat" was not the word that came to mind in contemplating him. Sitting perfectly still, with only those distinctive eyes in perpetual motion, he merely gave the impression of a powerful machine at rest. At any moment it might rumble into life, crushing anything in its path.

"I take it we are about to 'cry "Harry" '?" said Holmes, peering into his whisky.

"I have already 'let slip the dogs of war,' " his brother replied.

Observing the two of them together was like being a spectator at a tennis match. Each was capable of completing the other's thought and leaving any third party wallowing in their wake. Fortunately, in my case, they were usually prepared to take pity.

"My lords and masters have come to the obvious but reluctant conclusion that we have some unfinished business on our hands. They are shocked that Daintry, who after all, was 'one of us,' should renege on a gentleman's agreement in this way."

(You will understand that for the reasons previously stated, I am still not at liberty to reveal the man's true name.)

Holmes gave a harsh, humourless laugh.

"The man can butcher innocent women but they still expect him to keep his word as a gentleman?"

Mycroft resembled nothing so much as a sphinx. It was clearly not an issue worth pursuing.

"But they do at least concede that this recent killing was his work—the work of 'The Ripper'?" Holmes continued.

"Reluctantly, they do—and that is why I have asked you to come here this evening. We have spent every moment of the past forty-eight hours combing the country for this man and our resources, as you might imagine, are by no means trifling. We have found not so much as a hair of his head, heard not so much as a whisper. As a result, I have persuaded the Prime Minister that you should be invited to take on the case in an official capacity—working, of course, with Scotland Yard."

"Naturally, and handing over any credit to them, should I prove successful. The old sweet song. But—"

He raised a hand to prevent Mycroft from saying anything.

"Naturally, I accept. And I would not be too sure about 'a hair of his head.' However, the case has its points of interest, does it not, Watson? It will give me great personal satisfaction to cut through the hypocrisy that has bedevilled this matter from the outset and to apprehend this pathetic man, whoever he may be . . . ."

"I take it, then, you believe . . . ?"

"I would stake my reputation and my gambling friend here . . . ." he nodded in my direction—"would, I am sure, be prepared to bet what is left of his army pension when the turf has finished with it, that the man we are looking for is anyone *but* Lord Daintry, the man who was unceremoniously—and, I might add, anonymously and illegally—deposited on French soil in November 1888. I know our French cousins have much to answer for over the centuries but . . . however, I digress . . ."

"Yes, Mycroft, a very dangerous man is in our midst and I doubt very much that he is here for the sake of his health—or anyone else's. Tell me about Lady Hatton. Unless I am very much mistaken, we have there the end of a thread that may unravel a whole tapestry?"

Was it my imagination, I asked myself, or was Mycroft uncomfortable for the first time?

He finished his drink and reached for the decanter, as he weighed his words.

"Nothing less than the death of Adeline Hatton could have persuaded the colleagues to take this matter seriously," he said, his eyes fixed on the tablecloth. "I'm afraid that is the sad fact of it."

"But why *her?*" I interrupted. "Surely this is just the Ripper finding one more woman to exorcise his madness?"

Mycroft raised those gray liquid eyes in my direction and seemed to see right through me.

"I'm afraid there is rather more to it than that, Doctor," he said.

"Sherlock, you will remember that when we 'tried' Daintry, we appointed a secret—'jury' is the only appropriate word for it?"

Holmes nodded.

"Even you were not given the details. There were three of them. Adeline Hatton was one."

In the silence that followed I could hear for the first time the faint clatter of hansom cabs in the street outside and the subdued sound of the crowds passing to and fro. We were within feet of the safe epicentre of civilisation and yet in this room evil hovered.

The spell was broken as Mycroft continued . . .

"It was decided that Daintry should be tried by his peers. He was, as you remember, Sherlock, a man of means, a philanthropist, even. He had no need to work but he sponsored some kind of clinic and I believe he dabbled as something of an amateur scientist. We always assumed that he picked up his so-called 'medical' knowledge in that way . . .

"Consequently, we chose a jury of professional people to determine what should be done . . ."

"Which could be called spreading the responsibility . . . ?" This from Holmes.

"Just so. Since all the crimes had been committed against women, the Home Secretary of the day felt that—with the growing importance of female opinion within our society . . ."

Mycroft shrugged his massive shoulders. It

was clear that this was an argument he had been through more than once in the past.

"So—Lady Adeline Hatton was one," said Holmes. "And the other two?"

"James Harcourt . . ."

"The 'Hanging Judge,' " I said without thinking.

"Correct, Watson, that pillar of penal rectitude. And the third?"

"Cyril Overtoil, the Master of Magdalen College, Oxford."

"I see. A divine balance. *Femina, Justitia, Academia*. And so it was done. And what now? Have the others been warned?"

"I sent Overton a telegram myself. I'm afraid that, like all academics, he lives in a world of his own. The man might as well run on tramlines, he is so inflexible in his ways . . ."

I had a mental picture of a pot and a kettle in animated conversation but I held my tongue, for I could see that Holmes was doing his best to restrain a smile.

"He has an important banquet at the college in two days' time and nothing must be allowed to interfere with that. He apparently has some rather special guests. He says that, although we are making a lot of fuss about nothing, he is perfectly prepared to discuss things once that is over and he has invited us to attend. I took the liberty . . ."

Holmes and I exchanged glances, then nodded our assent.

"And the Judge . . . ?"

"Well, as I'm sure you remember, Harcourt retired from the Bench two or three years ago. This year he accepted the honorary post of Director of Covent Garden . . ."

"Yes, I seem to remember adding that announcement to my index," Holmes said thoughtfully. "It seemed a rather bizarre appointment at the time."

"I believe the administrators felt that the place needed a firm hand on the tiller." Mycroft allowed himself the smallest of smiles. "Which it has certainly received.

"Harcourt has been out of the country for the past few days but I have been in communication with him this morning and he has agreed to meet us later this evening at the Opera House. They are opening a new production, I believe."

"Yes, Wagner. *The Flying Dutchman*. A friend of ours . . ."

A look from Holmes stopped me in mid flow but Mycroft appeared not to notice.

"I am most impressed, Doctor. I had no idea you were such an opera expert. But I believe you are right. It is a Wagner night. Not one of my favourites, though, I know Sherlock . . ."

"Indeed," Holmes interjected, "but I have developed a soft spot for Verdi lately, haven't I, old fellow?"

Mycroft rang the bell and, once the food had

been served and we were once again alone, we discussed the situation in more detail.

"Mycroft, these men must be made to realise that the Daintry who has returned is not the Daintry they sent into exile. Despite his method of disposing of Lady Hatton, he is no longer simply interested in punishing the female sex. I would wager that this time his fantasies are much grander, perhaps even grander than mere revenge on a few individuals. Though that, of course, must be our first priority."

Over the next hour we discussed various options, none of which seemed particularly promising. After all, what did we know? That Daintry no longer *called* himself Daintry, no longer *looked* like Daintry and was extremely unlikely to inhabit any of Daintry's old haunts.

"In short," Mycroft said, screwing up his napkin and tossing it on to the table, "we have no cards in our hand at this moment?"

"Well," said Holmes, "perhaps we have *one*. It might not be the ace. But I believe a Queen can catch a Knave."

"Holmes," I cried, hardly able to believe my ears, "surely you cannot mean . . . ?"

"Don't worry, old fellow, I of all people am not going to take undue risks in that quarter."

Then, in answer to Mycroft's raised eyebrow— "You have your secrets, Mycroft and we, for the moment, must be allowed ours. And now perhaps we should see if the Flying Dutchman has reached safe harbour. An excellent dinner. My compliments."

I murmured my own thanks as we passed from the private room and crossed the main dining area. As we had deliberately dined early, the room was not yet crowded and the subdued lighting played on the cut glass and damask of the table settings, picking out details of the elaborate decorations on screen and mouldings.

My eye was taking all this in, for I was not in the habit of frequenting the place often, when I heard a loud voice hail us.

"My dear Mycroft! How is the Dionysus of the Diogenes? The Puppet Master of the Powerful? And this, I take it, is your brother, the Super Sleuth of Baker Street, who bids fair to become almost as famous as I am. You *must* introduce us . . ."

Mycroft seemed to be embarrassed but there was little he could do but stop at a table occupied by two men. One of them was extremely large, except by comparison with Mycroft—well over six feet, I would have judged. His complexion was florid and his face, not to mention his body, spoke of considerable over-indulgence. Had I been his medical advisor, I should have had a serious word with him, although something in his assertive manner told me that he would have brushed it aside. He was carefully, even fastidiously, dressed in what I'm sure was the height of fashion, though it was far too *avant garde* for my taste.

Everything about the man seemed designed to call attention to himself. But then—perhaps because his attention was not focused on me and I was, therefore, able to study him more carefully—I noticed something strange. Although he was trying to give the impression of complete confidence and insouciance, this man was ill at ease. The eyes were flickering nervously round the room, as if to see who was witnessing his performance, and there was a distinct line of perspiration on his upper lip.

His companion was a much younger fellow, no more than in his early twenties, whereas the older man would not see forty again. He also was well dressed but in a much less ostentatious fashion and it was obvious that he deeply resented our presence. In fact, it seemed to me that we had been used as a diversion in an argument they had been having when we came into view.

Mycroft quickly filled the breach.

"Sherlock . . . Doctor . . . may I introduce Mr. Oscar Wilde and . . . ?"

"Lord Alfred Douglas . . . Bosie to his friends—on those intermittent occasions when he has any."

Lord Alfred merely frowned sulkily and made no effort to acknowledge our presence.

Wilde seemed to be determined that nothing should interrupt his flow.

"Detecting must be such a fascinating occupation, Mr. Holmes. It reminds me of my visit to the so-called United States, which I found to be anything but. They maintain that America was discovered but I always say that it was merely detected . . ."

"Yes, Oscar, that's quite right. You *always* say it—just like you always say *everything . . .!*"

The interruption was from Lord Alfred, who pushed his chair back from the table and rushed out of the restaurant, almost knocking over a waiter in his haste.

There was a sudden silence before the buzz of conversation resumed. For some reason I had the distinct impression that this was not the first time the Café Royal had witnessed such a scene. And I was equally certain that Oscar Wilde was positively relieved to see his churlish guest depart.

Wilde looked thoughtfully at the empty doorway.

"There are times when I have likened his slim gilt soul to the proverbial perfection of the lily but there are, increasingly, others when the rather more constricting convolvulus comes to mind."

Holmes spoke for the first time.

"Mr. Wilde, fascinating as I find your botanical

speculations, I'm afraid we have pressing business elsewhere."

But as we began to move on, Wilde pushed himself to his feet.

"In which you must permit me to join you. I have often thought that I would make an excellent detective. Find me a miscreant, Mr. Holmes, and I will guarantee to talk him out of his evil intent."

To the hovering *maître d'*—"Charge it to my account."

"Thank you, Mr. Wilde, but Lord Alfred has already done so . . ."

The news seemed to come as no surprise to Wilde, who linked his arms with those of Mycroft and Holmes and steered them firmly towards the door, allowing me to bring up the rear and observe the frankly relieved looks of the remaining diners.

I must admit that my emotions were somewhat mixed but the sight of the Holmes brothers rendered jointly speechless for what must have been the first time in their lives provided a moment to treasure.

Out in the street, to my surprise, a hansom was already waiting and the driver immediately touched his hat when he saw Wilde.

As if in answer to an unspoken question, Wilde said airily—"Oh; when I find I have a good cab, I tend to keep him all day. It saves all that subsequent gesticulation. Where to?"

"The Royal Opera House, Covent Garden," I said weakly.

The ride was a short one and within a few minutes we were bowling into Covent Garden. It was then that we noticed something strange. By rights the area should have been relatively quiet at this time of night. It had been arranged that we should meet Harcourt in his office after the curtain had risen. By now several hundred avid opera goers should be packing the hall and listening entranced to the strains of Richard Wagner's music. Instead they appeared to be milling around outside and, even from here, the atmosphere did not have the normal buzz of anticipation one normally associates with a pre-theatre crowd. These people were certainly excited but I could sense hysteria in the noise they were making.

"Hello," said Holmes, "isn't that our friend Lestrade?"

As we decanted ourselves on to the pavement, a flustered Lestrade rushed up and seized Holmes by the arm. Now I could see that a number of his men were trying to control the crowd and move them away from the doors of the opera house.

"Mr. 'Olmes . . . Doctor . . . I don't know when I've been more pleased to see the two of you . . . and you, too, of course, Mr. Mycroft, sir," he blurted out, totally ignoring Wilde—a fairly difficult feat, which he nonetheless accomplished.

"What is it, Lestrade?"

I had rarely seen Holmes so tense. "Is she . . . ?"

"*She?* There's no 'she' about it, Mr. 'Olmes. It's an 'im. I've never seen anything like it, straight I've not."

At that moment a cloaked figure ducked under the arms of two of the restraining constables and was at our side. The hood was pushed back and we were looking into the white and frightened face of Irene Adler.

I say "white" but that was not quite true. Although the woman was clearly fighting to control genuine fear, she was also wearing heavy stage make-up which created a melodramatic effect that was somehow totally in keeping with the maelstrom of madness that seemed to be surrounding us.

"Oh, Sherlock . . . John . . . I've been praying you would get here! Yes, yes, I'm fine." This in response to our anxious expressions.

Drawing her to the relative shelter afforded by the waiting hansom, Holmes sought to calm her.

"Take your time but try to tell us in your own words . . ."

"It was a strange evening," Irene began, "but I thought that was to do with me. I was feeling quite light-hearted after our talk this morning. After all, I had just this one performance to get through and all would be well, of that I was sure. Perhaps because of my own preoccupation, I missed something I would otherwise have noticed.

"Anyway, the curtain rose on the first act. There was the usual sort of stage business to set the scene in the harbour and then, quite early on, the Flying Dutchman's ship is meant to enter. The production is an elaborate one and the ship is almost a full size replica with the masts fully rigged. The stage hands have had quite a few problems in moving it during rehearsal, so all attention backstage was on the mechanics of the scene. As it enters, the sails are being furled—it is all very lifelike . . ."

She paused, as the memory came back to her.

"Take your time," Holmes said gently.

"And then, as the ship came into the audience's view . . . I heard a gasp, then someone screamed. From where I was standing I could see every-one looking up into the flies. I did so, too, and there . . ."

"Yes?"

". . . there was this man hanging from the top spar of the rigging. He was hanging there and just swinging to and fro like a rag doll . . . Then someone backstage must have seen what had happened and the curtain came down. The next thing I remember, the police were here and emptying the theatre. Remembering what you said, I rushed down and joined the crowd. I was afraid to go back to my dressing room, so I just snatched a cloak that was hanging on a peg backstage and . . ."

Wilde was the first to speak and for once he set aside the well-turned phrase.

"So some unfortunate stage hand . . . ?"

"I'm afraid not, sir . . . Mr. Wilde, isn't it?" Lestrade seemed to have recovered his own professional composure now. "No, that was our first thought, of course—until we were able to climb up a ladder by the side of the stage and take a closer look at the gentleman concerned. No, the victim is . . ."

"Mr. Henry Harcourt. Formerly Lord Justice Harcourt." Holmes spoke quietly but we all heard him clearly enough.

"And now quite decidedly 'late,' " Wilde added but the flippancy was missing in his tone.

And then Holmes did a surprising thing. Turning to Lestrade, he said—"I wonder if I could trouble one of your constables to go down to Printing House Square and fetch me an early copy of tomorrow's *Times*?"

Then, seeing that the Inspector was about to say something, he continued—"No, I realise it would be premature to expect an account of this evening's events, however garbled. All I require is the agony column. Thank you." This to the young constable, who saluted and rushed away.

As he did so, I happened to be looking past Holmes and Irene into the crowds. People were still swirling around in the apparently haphazard fashion of eddies in a pool but somewhere in the foreground a bright splash of colour caught my eye.

It was the strikingly blond head of a tall man. No, it was the head of the man who had been scrutinising us last night inside this very theatre—and who was doing so again. At least he was until he saw me looking at him. He held my gaze for a moment then turned away and began to make his way back into the thick of the crowd.

"Lestrade," I cried urgently. "That blond fellow just moving away over there. Who is he, do you know?"

"Oh, I can answer that, Doctor," said Wilde. "He is a new planet that has recently swum into our little orbit. One Mr. Cain—Janus Cain, if you can believe such an appellation. Personally, I am inclined to believe he is but a poor figment of his own imagination."

"So *that* is Janus Cain?" Mycroft looked thoughtful. "Self-styled High Priest of . . ."

". . . the Church of the New Apocalypse," Holmes finished for him, "and the latest addition to my Index for 'C,' Watson. Remind me to re-read the item when we return to Baker Street. But I am inclined to agree with Mr. Wilde that a certain air of theatricality tends to attach itself to someone who appropriates such an ambiguous set of names and initials."

"What do you mean, Holmes?" I said, genuinely puzzled.

"Well, old friend, I think you will find that Janus was an ancient Roman god, the keeper of doors and gates, the master of new beginnings, commonly represented with two faces—one in front and one at the back and, thus, all-seeing. And Cain, of course, was the jealous elder son of Adam and Eve, who did away with his brother, Abel . . ."

It was Wilde who now picked up the thread. Staring at the back of the retreating object of our speculation, he said, barely perceptibly—"The question is—is *this* Cain able? And to do *what?*"

"Nor," Holmes continued, "do I think it entirely coincidence that he chooses to adopt the two most famous initials in the western world . . . 'J.C.' . . . for 'Janus Cain' read 'Jesus Christ.' He would presumably have us believe he has been sent to address our sins . . ."

The six of us were a temporary oasis of silence in the hubbub all around us.

Then Holmes seized the moment.

"Come, Lestrade, we have work to do. Miss Adler will come with us. Watson, would you be so kind as to ensure . . . ?"

"You can count on me, Holmes. More than one of us can have eyes in the back of his head."

I thought I caught a lightning glance exchanged between the brothers before Mycroft said—"Too many chiefs—or do I mean chefs? I will take Mr. Wilde for a nightcap at my club and we will regroup first thing in the morning at Baker Street . . ."

I had visions of the exotic Wilde shaking the Diogenes Club to its stuffy foundations, since it was a founding rule of the establishment that any member caught speaking to another could find himself disbarred. As if reading my mind, Mycroft continued *sotto voce* . . .

". . . it will be interesting to see what happens when an irresistible force meets an immovable object. Goodnight, madam—gentlemen . . ."

As the two of them re-entered the cab—Wilde, I thought, rather reluctant to be missing the excitement but a Mycroft under full sail was not to be gainsaid—I heard him start to piece together his familiar persona.

"Religion—as I'm sure you know, my dear Mycroft—is the fashionable substitute for belief . . . just as scepticism is the beginning of faith . . . I have often thought of founding an order for those who *cannot* believe—a Confraternity of the Faithless. After all, why should organised religion have all the best tunes . . ."

And then the cab was out of earshot and we were making our way through the crowds with the aid of Lestrade's sturdy fellows. I scanned the crowd carefully but there was no sign of the mysterious Cain.

Jostled and buffeted, we finally secured the relative peace of the theatre lobby. I had done my best to protect Irene from those who recognised her and wished to speak to her. Inside we found a determined cordon of police preventing access to the auditorium. When they saw Lestrade, they parted ranks just enough to let us through, then joined hands again. Covent Garden had rarely seen a drama like this, even on its famous stage— not even on a Wagner night.

The double doors swung to behind us and we were in a different world. Before us acres of empty plush seats. What little sound there was echoed round the empty hall and it came from the stage, where a large sailing ship seemed to have beached itself.

The curtain had been fully raised and we could see the gantry and the platforms above the stage from which the scenery was suspended. Several men were being lowered in a cat's cradle, while others had climbed high up in the ship's rigging, all in an effort to reach the broken object that was hanging there. As we walked down the central aisle towards the stage, someone managed to loop a rope around the body and slowly it was lowered to the stage, as if in some elaborate pagan ritual. Ironically, its arrival there coincided with our own.

In life Harcourt must have been a veritable martinet. A small, dapper man with iron grey hair cut short and a small, neatly-trimmed moustache. His suit of expensive tweed would have been equally immaculate, had it not been for the rope that had been wrapped around his torso in a kind of harness, so that it could be snagged on the ship's rigging.

In death he looked—as Irene had suggested—like nothing so much as a child's rag doll, limp and without purpose. There would be no more harsh lectures or draconian sentences from this particular source.

As I examined the body at Holmes's suggestion, I could see that, once again, the throat had been cut and the signature "x" marked the spot on the victim's jaw. I turned from where I was kneeling to nod to Holmes and Lestrade, just as the young constable hurried down the aisle towards us and handed Holmes a folded newspaper.

We gathered around him as he quickly turned the pages to find what he was looking for. I confess I have rarely scanned the racing results with greater interest.

"Ah, here we are—as I thought . . ." Holmes folded the paper and tapped an item in the agony column. In the same place as we had seen for the item referring to Lady Hatton I read—

"HANGING JUDGE"

and beneath it . . .

"Judge not, that ye be not judged"
(Matthew 7:1)

As I contemplated it, I heard Holmes say— "And then there was *one*."

Beside me Lestrade was clearly baffled by this recent turn of events.

"But I don't see how . . ."

Holmes cut across him. "This event was carefully planned well in advance, Lestrade. We ought to know by now that our friend leaves few things to chance. Moreover, he wants us to *know* how clever he is. He feels he can afford to advertise what he is about and challenge us to stop him. So far, I must admit, he has the advantage of us. It is up to us to see that he does not retain it and take game, set and match.

"Lestrade, I think what remains to be done here falls within your department. Doctor Watson and I have other business to attend to, so if you will excuse us . . . ?"

As we made for an Exit that would lead us backstage, we could hear the relief in Lestrade's voice, as he began to deal with matters with which he felt more at home. I felt sorry for the many who would have to labour long and hard before they saw their beds this night.

As we made our way through the corridors

behind the stage, Holmes addressed himself to Irene, who seemed to have recovered her composure.

"Tonight's events make it even more imperative that you do not return to the theatre until we have brought these matters to a conclusion."

We had reached a sort of crossroads and Irene indicated a short corridor that ended in a *cul-de-sac*.

"The dressing rooms are along here. Believe me, I shall be as quick as I can!"

"Then Watson and I will wait here, where we can see if anyone tries to enter the corridor."

So saying, we took up our positions just around the corner, where we had an uninterrupted line of sight and we heard the tap-tap-tap of Irene's feet receding and the sound of a door opening and closing. Up and down the other corridors there was not a soul to be seen. Clearly the police had emptied the premises as soon as the tragedy had been discovered. Even now the usual occupants must be being questioned in some other part of the building.

"What do you make of it, Holmes . . . ?" I was just starting to say, when I heard someone whistling those six unmistakable notes, *Auprès de Ma Blonde*. Then—as if orchestrated in one of the performances for which the house was famous—in succession there was a woman's scream, followed by a man's laugh and the noise of a metal door being slammed shut.

"Irene!" I don't know if it was Holmes or I who shouted. It may have been both of us for all I can tell. We were around the corner and into the corridor that held the dressing rooms before the echoes had died away.

The corridor was empty, then a door at the very end on the left was thrown open and Irene Adler dashed out and threw herself into my arms. She was wearing a robe and her face was scrubbed clean of the stage make-up, leaving it white and strained. Even *in extremis*, though, her beauty was remarkable.

"He was here. He was here again! No, I'm fine," she said in answer to Holmes's concerned enquiry. "I didn't see him—but he must have been close by. And then I *heard* him . . . And he left these . . ."

Without turning her head to look at it, she indicated the door of what was presumably her dressing room. Before I could say a word Holmes was inside. My arm still around Irene, I approached the door more carefully.

Inside was the usual clutter that seems to be the inevitable accompaniment of any woman of my acquaintance. Expensive dresses were draped across every available surface, shoes littered the floor. I have never understood why the process of tending to feminine beauty involves such apparent unawareness of the chaos created along the way.

Then my eyes went to Holmes standing by the lady's dressing table. In the full size mirror I saw not only our own reflections—two orphans of the storm, a heavy-set middle-aged man and a slender frightened woman—but the brooding aquiline presence of Holmes, his long, thin fingers sifting through something on that surface.

Moving closer, I peered over his shoulder. It had once been a bouquet of white roses. Now they were fragments of petals and stems, which even I could see had been hacked to pieces in a frenzy. I felt that I would not have cared to run into whoever was expressing such savagery.

What was even more chilling was the blood. It was as though the thorns of the roses had wounded the giver at the moment of giving, for the petals were now liberally dappled with blood. I tried to shield Irene from the sight but I had no need to. Her head was resolutely turned in the other direction.

"Hello, what's this?"

Holmes separated something from the ruin and held it up. It was a cluster of stems bound together and, as Holmes held them up to the gaslight I could see a glint of gold. They were tied with several strands of blond hair!

Next to me there was the sound of Irene Adler catching her breath. We had all been so fixated by the desecrated flowers lying in a pool of light, for all the world as though they were playing a star's role—as, indeed, they were—that we had failed for the moment to observe something else.

On the mirror, scrawled in one of Irene's grease pencils, were the words—

SOON, MY SENTA—SOON!

The sight of them seemed to galvanise Holmes.

"Stay here, both of you!" he snapped and was out of the door in an instant. I drew Irene gently to the doorway of her dressing room and away from the carnage on the table. From there we could see Holmes hurry up one side of the corridor and back down the other, opening dressing room doors and finding them empty.

He passed us and approached the blank wall at the end of it and began tapping it all over. Even standing some feet away, I could tell by the sound that it was solid. There were no hidden doors or passages there.

"Do you know, Holmes," I said, as he walked slowly back towards us, "this reminds me of that bizarre business at the *Paris* Opera round the time you and I first met . . ."

"You mean the so-called 'Phantom of the Opera'?" he replied. "But, if I remember correctly, that gentleman's ambition was to *promote* the career of his chosen singer. In view of tonight's evidence, I don't think we can assume that *our* phantom presently harbours similar ambitions."

"But what does the message mean? That's the first time he's left one, surely?"

Irene nodded and pulled her wrap more tightly around her.

"He's calling me by the name of the character I play in *The Flying Dutchman*. Senta is the young girl who goes off with him at the end." A thought suddenly struck her and she shivered, even though the corridor was not cold. "And they both drown in each other's arms. He's saying he will be back for me."

CHAPTER SIX

"The man believes in symbols and portents. While he may still be able intellectually to distinguish between fiction and reality, he is happiest creating his own universe in which he rules. Moreover, he finds it easy to adapt coincidence to his own ends . . ."

"For example . . . ?"

"He could not have known that Irene Adler would return to London, but once she did, he chooses to believe that in some way he has made it happen. He could not have arranged for Covent Garden to stage *The Flying Dutchman*, but now they have, he equates himself with the Flying Dutchman, cursed by society and forced to roam restlessly until he can find safe harbour. But there is one important difference . . ."

"Which is . . . ?"

"He does not see himself as a helpless victim. Rather, he pictures himself as an avenging angel, superior to everyone else, sent here on some divine mission of retribution. It is that conviction which makes him even more dangerous, Watson."

Holmes sank back in his chair. We were in Baker Street and I don't know about Holmes but I had passed a fitful night after we had delivered Irene into the safe keeping of Mrs. Hudson's friend with a strict injunction not to move out of the immediate vicinity until we sent word or came to fetch her. From the mutinous expression on her face I was sure of two things. The lady had completely recovered her composure and was now extremely angry at the circumstances that had brought her to this pass. Second, I was by no means as sure as my friend seemed to be that someone as headstrong as she could be relied upon to take orders from anyone but I kept my council.

"And you think this fellow Cain is our man?"

"Every instinct tells me so, old fellow, but I have not a shred of proof in my hands. Here— see for yourself . . ." and he handed me the bulky scrapbook he had at his feet.

It was one of the "C" volumes and a slip of paper marked his place. As I began turning the pages, he began to fill his filthy old pipe with the plugs of tobacco he had carefully arranged on the mantelpiece from the previous day—possibly from *several* previous days. But on that I chose not to dwell.

CADWALLADER, Edward—the Chelsea swindler. Holmes had trapped him by coating a document with a distinctive cayenne pepper mixture, which had adhered to his cufflinks . . .

CAESAR, Julius . . . an article on obscure Roman crimes, paying special attention to genocide . . .

Ah, yes, here it was—

101

CAIN, Janus . . . High Priest of the Church of the New Apocalypse . . . etc., etc. The gist of the piece, taken from the gossip columns of one of the popular papers of the day, was that the charismatic Mr. Cain had recently appeared on the London scene, apparently out of thin air, although there was some unsupported speculation about his having previously been somewhere on the Continent. His Church of the New Apocalypse claimed to be a new and fundamental reinterpretation of Holy Writ. The writer—a woman—seemed to find the reek of fire and brimstone positively exciting. In fact, the whole piece resembled nothing so much as a cross between a theatre review for a melodrama and a fashion show. Much was made of Cain's exotic garb and appearance. The man was clearly every bit as much a social as a religious phenomenon.

"The man's nothing more than a damned matinée idol," I grunted, handing the volume back to Holmes. "In fact, now I come to recall, when I was playing billiards at the club with my friend, Thurston, he mentioned that his wife and several of her friends had been to some big 'rally'—if that's the word—he was holding at the Albert Hall, of all places. The Prince Consort must be turning in his grave but the ladies were, apparently, ecstatic and threatened to go to the next one, too . . ."

I don't know if Holmes had heard a single word I'd been saying. He quite often drifts off into a world of his own and I suspect this was one of those times.

"Daintry-Cain . . . Cain-Daintry . . . Janus . . . two faces pointing in opposite directions . . . good and evil . . . and he believes he has been born again as a reincarnation of Jesus Christ?"

Holmes turned in my direction and his deep-set eyes were burning with their own messianic zeal.

"Fascinating, old fellow, fascinating. For the first time since the departure of the late lamented Professor Moriarty, we have an opponent worthy of our mettle—or, in a sense, *two,* for I have no doubt that Cain—Daintry . . . call him what you will—now genuinely believes that whatever he does is at the direct behest of that vengeful God of the Old Testament. A fanatic with right on his side may have the strength of ten."

"But where does Irene fit into his vision?"

Holmes leaned even further back into his armchair and steepled his fingers before his face—a habit that denoted serious thought.

"As I have often remarked, Watson, the fair sex is your department but if I were to venture a guess . . ."

"Yes?"

". . . Daintry was clearly smitten with her in his previous incarnation, if I may so call it, and interest soon turned to obsession—as I'm told may often happen. Her vehement rejection of his tentative approaches then created an ambiguous reaction in him. I do not say that it drove him to murder those women but it may well have caused his feelings toward the sex to reach a point of crisis that then expressed itself in cathartic violence.

"Irene Adler became for him . . ."

"*The* woman?" I interjected, before I realised just what I had said.

Holmes gave me a quizzical look but I sensed he realised I had not intended a jibe of any kind.

"Just so, Watson—*the* woman. The one woman he could not have but *must* have. The years go by and, suddenly, she enters his new life, still without knowing who he is. What else is he to think but that they are intended for one another in some mystical sense—preordained? But now he is no longer Daintry alone but also Cain, she has, I suspect, taken on another role in his dementia. She is now someone he both loves and fears—some sort of . . ."

"High Priestess? 'She-Who-Must-Be-Obeyed'?" I had not read my Rider Haggard for nothing.

"Something of the sort," Holmes replied, having clearly missed the reference. "She belongs at his side, whether she is Irene, Violetta, Senta—or whoever. The fact of her own multiple identities may well be feeding his delusions.

They are both immortals, capable of constant renewal while the rest of us poor mortals . . ."

"But what now, Holmes?"

"That, I fancy, is what brother Mycroft is here to discuss."

In my concentration on my friend's speculations, I had not attended to the ring at the door, nor had I heard the tread ascending our seventeen stairs. The latter omission was entirely excusable, since Mycroft Holmes was remarkably light on his feet, as large men often are. Now he was virtually filling our sitting room which, under normal circumstances, I had never considered particularly small.

After the usual brief pleasantries had been exchanged, he turned to the matter at hand.

"There are some red faces in the corridors of Whitehall this morning, gentlemen, as you may well imagine."

"A more becoming colour, nonetheless, than the two grey ones lying in the mortuary," replied Holmes sardonically.

"Indeed, indeed." Mycroft would have looked uncomfortable, had he known how. "There is a sense that, in some small way, bureaucracy may have contributed to the deaths of these unfortunate people. I have been instructed that I—we—must take personal care of the third party."

"Cyril Overton?" I queried.

"The distinguished Master of Magdalen . . ."

"If the Master of that particular college may be so described," said Holmes. I had never been able to winkle out of him the name of his own *alma mater*, though his incredible intellectual arrogance made me strongly suspect Balliol.

Mycroft—whom I knew to be a Christ Church man—ignored the remark.

"Unfortunately, I can get no sense out of the man. His confounded Winter Banquet is to be held tomorrow night and apparently the academic mind is only capable of concentrating on one task at a time. Consequently, I have arranged for the three of us to travel up to Oxford tomorrow afternoon on the 3:45 train from Paddington and stay in college overnight. I trust that will not inconvenience either of you too much. I'm told they keep a very fair table and we shall, naturally, be seated on the High Table with the Master and his guests . . ."

"Who are?" from Holmes.

"Now, there works the hand of coincidence, my dear Sherlock. There are two, to be precise. One is our eloquent companion from last night who was, in his day, it appears, a distinguished scholar there. A double first in classics, no less. Legend has it that he was so brilliant in translating a passage from the Greek version of the New Testament during his *viva voce* examination that the examiners stopped him part way through. To which Wilde replied—'Oh, *do* let me go on. I want to see how it ends.'

"The other is . . ."

"Mr. Janus Cain."

Mycroft raised an eyebrow a millimetre or so in lieu of a question.

"I would have been surprised, under the circumstances, if it had been anyone else," said Holmes, and then proceeded to tell Mycroft the events of the previous evening and our deductions. I say "our," since Holmes has frequently remarked that it is by relating the events of a case to me that he is enabled to see the connections which lead to a solution and, if I am able to fulfil such a valuable function in the deductive process, who am I . . . ?

"So the man is taunting us and defying us to stop him from completing his purpose?" Mycroft said ruminatively, when Holmes had finished his narrative.

"Only in part. To do that he could have hidden in the shadows and struck silently. There need have been no Janus Cain. No, I very much fear that these revenge killings are only the settling of old scores, a species of *entracte* to the main performance . . ."

"But what *is* the main performance, as you call it?" I butted in. "Fellow arrives looking and acting like—well, like You-Know-Who . . ." With my upbringing I have never found it easy,

107

like some people, to take the name of the Lord in vain. "He sets up some tin-pot church and has lots of foolish middle-aged women swooning over him. No crime in that, as far as I can see. If there was, half the actors in London would be behind bars."

I sat back, rather pleased with what seemed to me to be a pithy summary of the situation. I have to say that there are times when Holmes can over-complicate things. Wood for trees and all that.

"Money?" Holmes looked at his brother.

"Not as far as we can ascertain. Frankly, that was my first thought, that the man was engaged in some sort of confidence trick to get people to invest in the promise of a featherbedded Life-to-Come. However, I am informed that, not only does Cain not solicit donations to this 'church' of his, but he absolutely refuses them."

Holmes was silent for a moment, his eyes fixed on the ceiling.

"But then Daintry, if I recall, was a man of some considerable wealth and your friends . . ." —he looked at Mycroft—"were kind enough to let him transfer it out of the country when . . ."

"Yes, I believe I did hear something to that effect . . ." Mycroft looked as though the conversation was taking a turn he would rather avoid.

"So," Holmes continued, "seven years of sensible—perhaps brilliant—investment would leave the investor quite independent financially. But the question remains—to do *what?* Perhaps Watson here will be able to tell us . . ."

"Me? But I've never even met the fellow. How can I . . . ?"

"No, old fellow, but you are about to." He reached a long arm down the side of his chair and fished out a crumpled morning paper, folded so that a display advertisement immediately caught the eye. He skimmed it in my direction. I caught it and read—

RECLAIM YOUR SOUL!
Brothers and Sisters, are you in torment?
Do you fear the Divine Retribution to come?
There is a way to be saved . . .

It went on in this way for several more lurid lines of what was, frankly, poppycock. If I remember, hellfire and damnation were invoked more than once. Then it meandered to the point.

There was to be a rally of the Church of the New Apocalypse that evening at a hall in West London. All were welcome. The High Priest, Mr. Janus Cain would cleanse all those sinners who truly believed . . . etc.

"Holmes," I expostulated, "do you seriously expect . . . ?"

Holmes fixed me with a glacial stare.

"My dear Watson, I have been meaning, as

a friend, to point out to you that your soul is beginning to look distinctly grubby. This may be the very answer . . ."

And then even he could not hold back a burst of that explosive silent laughter of his, which would frighten any number of maiden ladies in seaside resorts. Even Mycroft permitted himself something approaching a smirk.

"But, Holmes," I said, when he had sufficiently recovered himself, "I haven't been inside a church since the last time I was married."

"Nor will you this time, old fellow," he replied. "I think you will find that the Gospel According to Cain owes rather more to Bamum than to Matthew."

Then, as he saw Mycroft heave himself to his feet . . . "But, Mycroft, you have yet to tell us about the irresistible force meeting the immovable object . . ."

"Ah, yes, the clash of mighty opposites. It was not without interest. Unfortunately, no sooner had I taken our friend into the main room that I was forced to leave him there while I attended to some important government business that had unexpectedly arisen . . ."

"Late at night?" Holmes interjected laconically.

Mycroft ignored the interruption.

"I am told on reliable authority that Mr. Wilde then spoke to the room at large for twenty uninterrupted minutes. He congratulated them on the room's *décor*, which he termed the *nouvelle nostalgie* school of architecture, then contrasted it with the barbarism he had found on his tour of the United States of America—a subject that seemed to strike a positive chord with the members, who cheered him to the echo, particularly when he asked them how one could trust a race that ignored the dado.

"As he left he told me they reminded him of the miners he had met in Colorado, though not, of course, so beautifully dressed, and he would like to commend them—as he had been commended himself—as being 'bully boys with no glass eyes.' With that, he climbed into his cab and bade me goodnight. Oh, and he added that if we needed any further help with our detecting, we were not to be afraid to seek his assistance . . ."

CHAPTER SEVEN

Soon after Mycroft had taken himself back to his Pall Mall lair—and with Mrs. Hudson fidgeting to tidy the room—Holmes and I betook ourselves to our respective bedrooms to complete our morning toilet. We had arranged to take Irene for lunch. "I see, gentlemen," she had said with a smile, "a temporary release for good behaviour?" Nonetheless, the idea had seemed to please her.

As it was a crisp, dry morning, we decided to walk.

It is so easy to take this great city for granted. Too often we hurry through it, our minds on the matters of the moment that are concerning us, and fail to really see it. Or else that fickle fellow, the Clerk of the Weather chooses to blanket it in mist or rain, so that its vivid charm is obscured.

Today, for some reason, all the right portents were in place. The sun shone and was reflected from shop windows, where a veritable cornucopia of merchandise from every corner of our mighty Empire was on show. Neatly-garbed servant girls pushed children in perambulators, middle-aged couples seemed to take their time as they strolled arm in arm and allowed those who were younger—and always seem to be in a hurry—to weave between them. Children dashed hither and yon, playing those inscrutable games, the rules of which are a secret known only by the very young.

I found it quite an uplifting sight but I had supposed that I was alone in my particular observation of it, when Holmes spoke.

"You know, old fellow, the human condition is a strange one. When Shakespeare wrote of all the world being a stage, he spoke truer than he could possibly have known. At this very moment we are wandering through one of its sets, brightly lit and full of hope. But if some celestial Stage Manager were to whisk it away, remove the roofs from the houses behind it and permit us to peer in, we would see such a mixture of good and ill, kindness and bigotry, mirth and malice as would provide the stuff of a million plays.

"We, Watson, spend so much of our lives with our noses pressed up against the window of crime and depravity, it is easy to miss the other view. But this . . ."—and with his cane he indicated the bustling scene around us—"this is also what people are capable of being, what the vast majority of them aspire to be. It is to permit them to fulfil those aspirations that we must continue to do our puny best to contain the forces of Evil."

Rarely have I heard him in such philosophic vein and I was moved to be shown a glimpse of that great heart he tries so hard to hide. He once said of me that he never got my limits, that I had—how did he put it?—"unexplored possibilities" about me. How much truer, I felt, was that observation about *him?*

Then—as if consciously righting some balance—he said . . .

"I think devilled kidneys. What about you?"

Mrs. Turner's house was in an undistinguished but neatly-kept side street just behind Covent Garden. As we picked our way between the discarded crates and cabbage stalks that were the relics of the morning market and avoided the porters with their heavy trolleys, I noticed that Holmes was carefully scanning the locality. I began to do the same.

As far as I could tell, we did not appear to be the object of anyone's undue attention but on that crowded canvas, who could be sure?

Soon we were plying a polished brass knocker.

I won't say we knew Mrs. Turner well but over the years she had occasionally stood in as housekeeper for her friend, Mrs. Hudson, when that good lady was visiting various members of her far-flung family. Consequently, she knew our little ways perfectly well and had learned not to ask unnecessary questions. In her turn she had deduced that there was usually a degree of method in our apparent madness.

When the door opened, it was not Mrs. Turner but Irene who stood there, though over her shoulder I could see the landlady hovering protectively in the background.

Gone was the bedraggled, though strangely beautiful, creature of the night before. In front of us was a lady from a fashion plate. With her close-fitting satin dress in a becoming shade of brown, a cloak in contrasting fabric but identical colour draped casually from her shoulders and a small white hat that appeared to have been artfully (and expensively) teased from nothing, she literally took one's breath away.

"You look beautiful, Irene," I said quietly, as I took her outstretched hand. But, having accepted my tribute with a genuine smile of thanks, it was obvious whose approbation she really wanted.

"Sherlock?" she said. In what might equally well have been a greeting or a question.

And then Holmes cleverly defused the moment.

"I see that you have slept well, patronise Fauché in the Rue St. Honoré, have shopped at Gorringes in the past twenty-four hours, accompanied Mrs. Turner to the Market this morning and are now ready for your lunch. Other than that, I can deduce nothing."

Not being used to my friend's parlour tricks, Irene Adler reacted as I have seen so many people react over the years. The eyes first reflect disbelief, then a touch of fear and finally, amazement. The latter phase is often accompanied by a slight but distinct gaping of the mouth.

In Irene's case the latter was caused by the fact that she was laughing as though she would never stop.

"Sherlock Holmes!" she cried as she took us both by the arm and literally dragged us into Mrs. Turner's cosy little sitting room. "You really are the devil they say you are. Now, you explain that to me before I strike you with my parasol."

"Which you have 'borrowed' from Covent Garden, incidentally," said Holmes, now positively enjoying himself, as he perched on one of the landlady's "best" chairs that only saw service on "special" occasions such as this.

"Oh, dear, Watson, I fear my reputation, such as it is, will be in shreds and patches, if I cannot break the habit of explaining things."

He turned to face Irene.

"The parasol, I admit, is accidentally obvious. You were twirling it coquettishly for an hour or so the other evening as Violetta. Like any other man in the audience, I could scarcely have failed to notice it . . ."

Irene nodded solemnly, as if conceding him one point.

"Fauché? The gown, if I may say, fits you so well, it is clearly not bought—what is the expression, Watson?"

"Off the peg?" I offered.

"Precisely. Moreover it has several features in

its design, such as the draping of the material over the left shoulder, that are signatures of Fauché. The Paris designer is beginning to have as many distinguishing signs as a painter has brush strokes. I suspect that M. Fauché has a dummy in his work room made in your image—but that, I admit, is speculation.

"The gloves were the subject of a special one day sale held yesterday by the Messrs. Gorringe and advertised in yesterday's newspapers. You have, by the way, omitted to remove their tag."

There was a small gasp from Irene and she looked down at her hands. Holmes, I noticed was looking decidedly smug.

"As for the Market, it is hard to ignore the basket of fresh produce on the table there, which I was able to see from the doorway. It was unlikely, under the circumstances, that Mrs. Turner would leave you alone in the house and further corroboration is provided by the cabbage leaf—no, I am in error . . ."

And with his cane he spiked a small green leaf from the side of Irene's tiny shoe.

". . . by the Brussels sprout leaf adhering to your shoe. You see, every mystery is simple, once it is explained."

Irene looked at him with a frown. "But you have omitted one highly significant detail, Holmes."

Holmes looked surprised. On these occasions

he is accustomed to servile surprise. I have never known his explanations questioned. "And what may that be, pray?"

"My readiness for lunch."

"Simply a wild guess!" Holmes replied. "Based on Watson's knowledge of women on three Continents." And the small room rang with our laughter.

Rules in Maiden Lane—a few short steps from the daily maelstrom of Covent Garden—is reputedly the oldest major restaurant in the City of London, dating back, I believe, about a hundred years.

Its distinguished history notwithstanding, it has always seemed to me a haven of civilised calm and never more than today, as we were shown to a table in a distant alcove, where we could see without being seen. All around us was dark polished wood, bevelled glass and comfortably worn plush. The world in which one might kill or be killed was far away.

"Here am I wearing my finest finery and you tuck me away from sight. Are you ashamed to be seen with me, Sherlock Holmes?"

Then she became serious and stayed his answer.

"It is so good to see you both. What has happened since I saw you last?"

Those remarkable blue eyes never left

Holmes's face, as he told her of our conversation with Mycroft and my plan to attend Cain's rally that evening.

"So you are convinced that this man is behind everything that has happened—then and now? And yet you can do nothing?"

"I am as certain of it as I am that there will be jugged hare on the menu they are about to bring to us. I am equally certain that this time there is a greater purpose behind his actions and his desires than mere bloodlust—and we must find out what that is. The man is clever and supremely confident. He believes himself to be invulnerable. Make no mistake about it, in some demented way he believes the Lord is on his side.

"Were we to take him into custody, he would simply laugh at us and bring in some expensive lawyer to accuse us of hounding an unorthodox servant of God. Can you not imagine the headlines? Lady Hatton's organisation, for one, would be on us like a ton of bricks . . ."

"Not the happiest of allusions, Holmes, if I may say so," I interjected.

"Just so, Watson, just so. You see how I need my Watson to keep me honest?

"Cain, too, has his own organisation and its purpose is not to save souls. No, this time he means to leave his mark—the mark of Cain—on all of us and I fear we have little enough time to discover where he plans to leave his brand."

There was a natural silence at the table, while the aproned waiter hovered and took our order.

When he had departed, Holmes told her something of our future plans.

"We have allowed this man to dictate events so far but it is now time for him to be thrown off course. It will be interesting to see how a man who believes himself to be God reacts when that divine right is challenged."

"So do you intend to disrupt this evening's rally?" Irene asked.

"By no means. I merely desire Watson to observe Cain in action and report back. I myself have been summoned to an emergency meeting with Mycroft and his colleagues, though I have few expectations in that direction. No, my old friend here has, as so often, the more enviable task."

I thought of some of the "more enviable tasks" I had been given over the years, several of which had turned out to be a distinct risk to life and limb, but this hardly seemed the moment to debate the point.

Some time later, with the winter light fading and the lamps being lit, we delivered Irene back into the safe keeping of Mrs. Turner, promising to keep her informed on a daily basis of the progress we were making.

She looked, I thought, a little sad to see us go. As we turned the corner of the street, I looked back. She was still standing at the open door and watching.

CHAPTER EIGHT

The Croxley Hall in Hammersmith had passed through a number of incarnations in its time. It had begun life as a warehouse for storing grain, then been converted into a community theatre. Now it was available for hire by any group for any purpose. If I'm not mistaken, the last time I had had cause to pass it, it was hosting a World Conference of Numismatists.

Certainly, it can have seen nothing more exotic than The Church of the New Apocalypse.

One had to give Cain his due. In a few short months he had spread his word widely and, by the looks of the people streaming towards the shabby edifice from every direction, that word seemed to have fallen on receptive ground.

There were the usual anonymous looking folk, who seem prepared to turn out for any kind of gathering, from a road accident to a rally, and have nothing better to do. But there were working class families, often with children in arms, and more than a sprinkling of well-to-do matrons, who seemed surprised to find themselves in these unaccustomed surroundings but who, nonetheless, stepped carefully from their carriages and hurried into the hall.

I had taken care to arrive a little early myself for the very purpose of watching the crowds and, as the minutes ticked by before the event was due to begin, I confess I was becoming increasingly puzzled and concerned. Were these people here today in expectation of some kind of circus spectacle? Somehow I didn't think so. There was not the subdued buzz of excitement one detects in the approach to Sanger's big top, for instance. Instead, there was a sense of concentration and expectancy. They felt they were about to hear something important. I could only conclude that a considerable number of our fellow citizens felt the need to be saved.

I was also struck by the attendants who were guiding the congregation to their seats. To a man they were young and well-muscled and dressed in identical black suits—a far remove from the elderly folk who had shuffled around the pews in our local church when I was a boy. If they were typical of the servants of the New Apocalypse, Cain did not have followers; he had recruited a militia.

Now the attendants were beginning to close the doors of the hall. I hastened across the road and slipped inside, taking a seat in the back row on one of the shabby cane chairs that threatened to impress itself on my person long before the evening was over.

As I was striving to find a comfortable position,

I was vaguely aware of a commotion at the door. A few latecomers were insisting on being let in and I heard one of them complain in a loud tone about "the door of the House of the Lord standing ever open."

A moment later I was being urged to move up and make room and happily bequeathed my seat to a shabby Nonconformist clergyman, whose suit looked as though it could have done with a good dusting.

Next to him on the very end of the row was a voluminous old lady, who had apparently done her week's shopping on her way here and was now experiencing considerable difficulty in finding a place to stow all her packages, not to mention her umbrella.

What an ill-assorted group we must have made, I thought, as two of the black-suited young men firmly placed their backs against the closed doors.

At that moment there was the sound of a trumpet, even though the simple stage at the end of the hall was completely bare, except for a single chair.

The disembodied quality of the sound and the fact that it seemed to be coming to us through some kind of amplification made it echo around the hall, which immediately fell silent. By the excited expressions I could see on many faces, as people turned to seek the source of the sound, they seemed to wonder if they were hearing the Last Trump.

And while they were disconcerted, a small door at the back of the platform opened and closed and Janus Cain was in our midst.

I had to admit, it was cleverly staged. A trap door could not have been more effective. The man carried a heavy candelabra, which he set beside the chair and the wavering flames played up and across his face, giving it an unearthly appearance.

There was the full face with its thin lips, the cascade of hair and beard that I had seen so recently, the piercing black eyes that seemed to pick out each member of his audience, as though he could see into their very souls.

I heard the clergyman next to me muttering to himself. As far as I could catch it, he was saying something about "Vanity of vanities. All is vanity." It was, I must confess, a sentiment with which I was beginning to agree whole-heartedly.

I was about to whisper as much when a sudden thought struck me and I took another sidelong look at my neighbour.

The disreputable black suit, the pinched, furrowed face, the lank, greasy hair . . . they were all very familiar, now that I came to look closer. Baker Street. Of course. How many times had I seen Holmes adopt that particular guise and sally forth, so that he could pass freely among the lower elements of our great city? And he thought he could deceive me with it one more time?

"Don't worry, Holmes!" I muttered, digging him in the ribs for his pains. "Mum's the word." He started to say something about bearing false witness against one's neighbour—and then Cain began to speak . . .

Whatever you thought of the man, he was a mesmeric speaker, that had to be admitted. The public voice, at least, was low and vibrant. It seemed to echo off the walls of the old building and fill it.

He spoke of the ungodliness of the world we had all been sent to share. He told personal little parables of man's inhumanity to man. Whether they were true or not was immaterial, for he crafted them so skillfully that I could hear women whimpering all around me.

As he continued, the tone of his voice grew slowly but perceptibly higher and louder, as though what he was hearing himself say was angering him. I realised early on that he was employing the same tactic as I had read about with certain American fundamentalist preachers in backward areas. He was slowly but surely whipping this crowd up to an emotional frenzy.

Now a new element entered his discourse. Every now and then he would ask rhetorically— "Do you *hear* me?" At first his listeners did not appear to know how to respond but then there would be a loud cry of "We hear you!" The second time I was able to identify the source as the black-clad supporters, now acting as a *claque*.

Soon a number of the genuine congregation had enthusiastically got the point. "We *hear* you!" they cried and one or two even added "Hallelujah!" for good measure.

It was a bizarre spectacle to be taking place in the heart of the most civilised city in the world and it seemed to be particularly upsetting to my neighbour, who was now muttering about taking the name of the Lord in vain so loudly that he received a sharp "Ssh!" from the old lady on the other side of him.

"My dear Holmes," I felt like saying to him, "you are in severe danger of overplaying your hand." But, of course, I did not.

Cain was now moving into a higher gear in his address.

We were all of us blood-stained sinners. Our souls were besmirched, begrimed and forfeit. The Lord had been watching us and the Lord was sorely disappointed by what he saw. No, the Lord was now *angry* with his children. " 'Vengeance is mine,' He says. 'Vengeance and Retribution. . . .' "

In the back of my mind even I knew that he was using the line out of context but the familiar words were undoubtedly having their effect. Some people were now sobbing out loud, quite

127

oblivious to those around them. There was now palpable fear in that hall.

Cain paused and waited until the sound died down.

The Lord had come to him, he told us. The Lord had come to him and told him there had to be a new Beginning and that he was to be the Servant of the Lord who should be his Minister at this time of New Beginning.

" 'You will take a new name,' He told me. 'Henceforth you will be called Janus, for you will be all-seeing. And I name you Cain, for the days of gentleness and mercy are past. Before I grant a new world of Peace and Love, there must be great Cleansing. There shall be a New Apocalypse. I shall send the Four Horsemen— Pestilence, Famine, War and Death. Few will be saved to see that New World but you, Janus Cain, shall show them the way . . .' "

And then I swear the hair rose on the back of my neck, for in that dimly-lit hall a vision slowly took shape over Cain's head. It was like an engraving from some old tome. It showed four figures out of a nightmare. They were presumably men, though they wore cloaks that surrounded their heads, so that only their goblin eyes gleamed through, and they rode black steeds straight from Hell that reared up as if to stamp us all underfoot. And the image *moved*.

They got closer and closer. I could see the

breath from the horses' flaring nostrils and in my head I could hear the beat of those ghostly hooves.

The hall erupted in pandemonium. People screamed and a few appeared to have fainted. Several made a dash for the doors but were restrained by the servants of Cain, who sought to calm them. They alone seemed to be unsurprised.

And then—as suddenly as it had appeared—the vision was gone and when I looked at the stage, so was Cain. Only the candelabra—its candles much shorter now—guttered by the empty chair. Then, in what can only have been an accidental piece of orchestration—or was it?—the candles, too, were snuffed out in a gust of wind. The producers of that *Grand-Guignol* theatre the French were all talking about could have learned several valuable lessons from the events of this evening.

Now the doors of the hall were dramatically opened and the night air and the comforting lights of the street outside brought in a welcome touch of the everyday. People began looking at one another a little sheepishly, I thought, but there could be no doubt but that Cain had metaphorically made his mark. They would remember the man and his message and some would undoubtedly take it to heart.

One exception was the man at my side. "He hath paid no regard to the word of the Lord," he muttered and then added, as if in explanation, "Exodus. Nine. Twenty-one."

I chose not to dignify it with an answer. Since it would not do for us to be seen to be leaving together, I busied myself with my shoelace and, when I looked up, thankfully, he had vanished.

The crowds were streaming out by now, talking animatedly for the most part, though a few looked positively subdued. I heard a couple of society ladies saying, as they passed me . . .

"Do you know, dear, I felt a genuine *frisson*—and that's something one never gets with the Reverend Rowley . . ."

To which the other replied—

"Such a *manly* man. Do you think he could be persuaded to address . . . ?"

Outside stood Cain greeting the departing guests—some of them by name. It was clear that some of them were regular attenders at these little *soirées*. I noticed that two of his attendants stood a little behind him holding flaming torches—the fires of Hell?—which just happened to throw a light that created a halo effect around that golden head.

As I approached the doorway, I could see that Cain was in earnest conversation with a young man who had clearly been much affected by the events of the evening. Although I could not hear what the man said, it obviously pleased Cain, who gave deprecating little shrugs.

I made a mental note. Brown suit of foreign cut. Soft brown hat pulled well down—similar. Slim build. Round spectacles. Long but rather wispy moustache. Age—around thirty.

Their conversation interrupted by other departing members anxious to have a word with this new Messiah, the young man wrung Cain's hand warmly, waved a hand in salutation and hastened off into the night.

His place was taken by the old lady, who had been seated on my row. Clutching her packages to her, she embarked on an incomprehensible eulogy. What a revelation . . . she had never in her whole life . . . divine intervention.

Cain smiled and smiled but it was obvious that this was not the object of his exercise and, after a minute or two of this, I saw him nod to one of his henchmen, who moved up to the old lady and tried, without making it too obvious, to move her along.

Unfortunately, he only succeeded in jostling her arm and, before anyone knew quite how it had happened, her bags were strewn all around her and the contents rolling around the pavement— bread, candles, vegetables and who knew what else.

Cain could scarcely contain his irritation. His plan was to play the benevolent saviour and this was no part of it. His eyes flashed instructions to his acolytes and they hurried to clear up the mess.

I decided to take advantage of the confusion to make my departure but, as I sidled around the debris, I heard Cain's voice call out—

"Goodnight, Doctor Watson. So glad you could join us."

CHAPTER NINE

I must admit that I was not in the best of moods with Holmes and my irritation was not improved by the fact that a light rain had begun to fall, for which I was not prepared. The Croxley Hall, moreover, was situated in a street in the back of beyond and I had to walk for fully a quarter of an hour before I could find a cab.

Once safely ensconced in the dry, I reviewed the evening's events. Why had Holmes pretended he had another appointment, sent me off in his stead and then turned up anyway? Why send the dog and bark yourself? It was not the first time this had happened. No, I should definitely have a word on the matter with Mr. Sherlock Holmes.

But, I determined, that word could wait. On the way home I would drop into the club for a drink. After all, this damp night air . . . purely medicinal reasons. I instructed the driver accordingly and immediately felt better that I had acted so decisively.

No sooner had I put my head round the door than I was grabbed by young Thurston. Well, I say "young," though he must be my age. It's just that somehow one's contemporaries never seem to get any older.

"Come to relive your humiliation, Watson?" he called out.

"My . . . ? Oh, you mean billiards?" He'd been a trifle lucky at our last encounter. "Sorry, no, old man. Urgent business. Only time for a swift one . . ."

And then one thing led to another and I found myself telling him about the rally. Then he began telling me about the way his wife and her friends had taken to following Cain and his troupe around the London area. They thought it a rare evening out. Some of the tales they came back with made this evening pale.

Apparently, when the frenzy was really on him, Cain would call for people in the congregation who were in some way disabled to come forward and be cured. Mrs. Thurston claims they had seen some amazing sights and wouldn't hear a word against him. "If the people who supposedly ran this country did a fraction as much as Janus Cain, we should all be a lot better off," was a sentiment frequently to be heard in the Thurston household, it would seem.

Hearing us talking brought in old Archie Sennott, who's something high up on one of the papers—I forget which—and he said that his paper had tried investigating some of these "cures."

"And do you know, my people could never lay a hand on *one* of them. Seemed to be spirited away but, you know, I'd lay a pound to a penny that some of them would turn up another night looking different and go through it all over again.

"But what's even more interesting," he went on, "are those lads he surrounds himself with. We've had a bit more luck checking some of them out and most of them have got 'form'—served time for rough stuff, that sort of thing. Suppose Cain feels he needs protection from the likes of Mrs. Thurston and her friends . . . !"

It was with renewed spirits that I returned to 221B an hour or so later. I had covered more ground than Holmes could possibly have imagined and gleaned some valuable insights.

I ran into Mrs. Hudson in the hallway.

"Oh, Doctor, Mr. Holmes isn't back yet but I didn't think you'd be long, so I showed the young man up to the sitting room. He said he didn't think you'd mind."

"Well, that depends on who he happens to be, Mrs. Hudson," I said jovially, for I had begun to feel well-disposed towards life in general. "Do we have any further clues?"

As she disappeared into her own quarters, I thought I heard her say over her shoulder— "American gentleman, by the sounds of him."

I entered our sitting room and went over to the coat rack to hang up my ulster, still damp from earlier in the evening. Out of the corner of my eye I discerned a slender figure sitting in the visitors' basket chair.

"Good evening," I said. "Sorry you've been kept waiting. I observe you are from America. Which part of America?" *Holmes should see me now,* I thought, *I've seen him impress people with less.*

"Let's say—Cleveland," was the reply.

It was then that I had my first real look at the speaker and I stopped in my tracks. It was the young man I'd seen after the Cain rally. Same brown suit, same soft hat. The long moustache, much fuller than most young men were wearing. What was he—twenty-eight? Thirty?

"Let's *say* Cleveland, Doctor. For no one in their right mind would admit to New Jersey. Oh, I beg your pardon—you must think me extremely rude . . ."

And with that he swept off his hat and a cascade of blonde hair fell around his face.

I found myself looking at a moustachioed Irene Adler . . .

"But I . . ." I began, when Irene raised a finger to her lips. There was a step on the stair, as someone began to climb towards our room.

Hastily, she began to pile her hair back under the hat and now I could see why she had chosen one so large and shapeless. In a moment the young buck had returned.

Now I determined to get something of my own

136

back. As the footsteps reached the door and the handle began to turn, I called out—"Come in, Reverend. Or do you need a little help?"

The door swung open—and there, her arms still full of bags and parcels, was the garrulous old lady.

"No, thank you, Watson, I think I can manage," said Sherlock Holmes.

Then, as he let his various impedimenta fall to the floor—"Good evening, Irene. That shade of brown is most becoming."

Now it was Irene's turn to look stunned. Once again she removed the hat and this time pulled gingerly at her moustache.

"I think you will find just the smallest dab of Leichner's adhesive will do the trick in future," Holmes continued, as though he were commenting on the weather.

"You once told me that male costume was nothing new to you, since you had been trained as an actress. It was a remark I have never forgotten. Even so, it took me some while to see you, I who know your face better than most and am trained to see through a disguise. In future, be careful of the eyes. The windows to the soul, so they say. It's something I can never impress upon Watson."

And he began to remove his own trappings of wig, bonnet and shawl. I threw him a handy towel and he began to rub the make-up from his face.

Bit by bit the lean, laconic features of Sherlock Holmes reappeared.

What a strange trio we must have looked.

"And you, Watson. I don't know what that unfortunate clergyman must have thought. Assailed by the ravings of a maniac from the platform and the nudgings and winkings of a questionable military man from the side, I expect he rushed straight home to consult the Good Book."

Personally, I didn't see much humour in the situation but, since the other two certainly did, I was forced to join in. The man *had,* after all, looked remarkably like a startled rabbit, now I came to think of it.

I also felt considerably better when Irene admitted that she, too, had drawn the same conclusion.

"I could have sworn it was the same bumbling old cleric you used on me all those years ago, when you were trying to prise that stupid photograph from me at Briony Lodge. 'Shame on you, Sherlock Holmes,' I thought, 'for showing so little imagination.' Everyone who has read John's tales in the *Strand Magazine* must look at every stray vicar and think—'There goes Sherlock Holmes!' "

Holmes smiled in an abstracted way. He was obviously still reliving the recent experience.

"That fellow who was organising the rest.

I knew I'd seen him before, Watson. Thin features and a most villainous appearance. Raoul Sugarman. Down Hoxton way they call him the Raging Rabbi due to his vicious temper. I very much fear that we are dealing with a very ugly group of customers indeed."

Then, just as quickly, his mood changed again and he was back with us.

"But I have no doubt that three such redoubtable musketeers as our good selves will prevail."

Mrs. Hudson having by now retired for the night, I busied myself preparing a hot drink for us all, as Holmes—or Mrs. Bagshaw, as he insisted on calling himself—stoked up the fire.

"Come, old fellow, admit it—I was never more convincing. That baggy parasol that kept stubbing itself on Cain's toes . . . a touch of genius!"

When we were comfortably seated, Holmes fixed Irene Adler with one of those penetrating looks of his that I am always grateful to see turned on someone else.

"And now, young lady—an explanation, if you please . . ."

"First of all, bless you for 'young,' " said Irene in a tone that would have made me feel I had no wish to ask a single question more.

"Perhaps the excellent lunch had something to do with it," she went on, "but after you had left me, I got to thinking about how intractable this problem seemed. Here we are, knowing who is doing all this and yet unable to prove anything. The man has built himself an ivory tower on his so-called religion and can hide within it whenever he likes.

"So I decided to storm that castle—or, at least, infiltrate it. Meet Ned Walsh, lay preacher from Cleveland, Ohio . . ." She indicated the hat and the costume. "I'm a simple kind of guy, sir . . ." and now the accent was unmistakably American—"and I know when the Good Lord is calling ma name. I heard him calling me tonight in that there hall, Reverend Cain, and when that New Apocalypse comes, I shall be ready!"

The young woman was, indeed, quite an actress. Then her tone changed yet again and this was a woman speaking from the heart.

"Sherlock, I know what you are going to say. Believe me, I have rehearsed all the arguments over and again. But you must understand that this is *my* life this man is taking over and I allow *no one* to do that. I intend to take it back. I intend to do that by removing Irene Adler from where he can see her and placing her where she will be quite invisible—right under his nose. The leaf in the forest.

"This evening after—after whatever that spectacle was—I introduced myself. I told him I wanted to study his methods and take the Word back to the States—To cut a long story short, he has invited me to the Janus Cain Temple.

He apparently has a complex of buildings in Whitechapel that he makes his headquarters . . ."

"Whitechapel, eh?" I said. "Surely, that's where . . . ?"

"Where the Ripper operated in his heyday. Precisely, Watson. Now, why, I wonder . . . ? But pray continue, Irene . . ."

"I may well discover nothing but at least it is better than sitting around, waiting for him to come to me, as I know he will."

"And your mind is totally made up?"

"Totally."

"Then let me make one proviso." Holmes leaned forward like some giant bird of prey about to take flight. By the way his fingers were pressed together, so that the knuckles shone white, I knew he was controlling himself with difficulty.

"You are, as you say, a free agent and Watson and I would have you no other way. What you contemplate is extremely dangerous. With your permission I shall have you watched night and day by the Baker Street division of the police force . . ."

"But that would defeat the whole purpose . . . !" Irene exclaimed.

"I don't think you quite understand Holmes's meaning," I interrupted with a smile, "not until you see the 'division.' My friend's private police force normally goes by the more colourful name of the Baker Street Irregulars . . . They are the most disreputable-looking gang of street urchins you have ever laid eyes on . . ."

"And not one of them stands an inch over four-feet-six," Holmes continued with a laugh, "yet I'll wager there's more useful work to be got out of one of those little beggars than out of a dozen on the regular force. It became obvious to me long ago that the sight of an official uniform seals men's lips but these little fellows are invisible. They can go anywhere, see everything, overhear any conversation—and they are as sharp as needles. You will never see hair nor hide of them but they will be your guardian angels.

"And now, old fellow, what did you make of this evening's events?"

"I have to admit, Holmes, that it was well managed, though it left a bitter taste that's still in my mouth. The man has the gift for rabble rousing, there's no doubt about that."

"He has that, right enough," Holmes mused. "There were moments there when I was reminded of what one reads of Robespierre and the worst excesses of the French Revolution. It only wanted one or two of those society ladies at the front to bring out their knitting. Yes, the psychology of the mob is a fruitful field for the talented fanatic. Today a few hundred people crowded into a suburban hall . . . tomorrow . . . Who can tell?"

"But the moving image, Holmes? How did he pull that off? I've never seen anything like it?"

"No, but you will, old fellow—and very soon. When I was taking my own—sabbatical—not too long ago . . ." and here he looked at Irene—"I spent some time in France, as you know . . ."

"Yes, studying coal tar derivatives in Montpelier or Montpellier or somewhere such . . ."

"In fact, I managed to wander a little further afield and found myself in Paris, where I made the acquaintance of the Lumière Brothers. The experiments they were making with what they were calling 'moving pictures' were quite fascinating and, from what I hear, a young apostle of theirs—young Georges Méliès—has now made a number of such images, which are becoming the talk of Paris. It is only a matter of time before they arrive on this side of the water. Meanwhile, it would appear that Daintry has made the same discovery and is now adapting it to his own ends . . ."

"You mean, the French are that far ahead of us?" I gasped.

"So it would seem." Holmes was clearly amused at my chauvinistic concern. "I'm afraid as a race we are inclined to think something should not be invented until we are good and ready to invent it ourselves. We are then duly put out when those of a different persuasion fail to share that perception. Now that our American cousins have—what is the phrase, Irene?—'the bit between their teeth,' too, I'm afraid you will

143

have to keep a careful watch over your blood pressure, old friend.

"Not to add to your travails, Watson, but Daintry/Cain was employing another little device that we may expect to encounter again in our line of work . . ."

"And that is . . . ?"

"His eyes . . ."

"What do you mean—his *eyes?*"

"That's right." It was Irene who was leaning forward now. "I've never seen anyone with eyes that colour . . ."

"And you never will," Holmes replied, "at least, not in nature. Our friend has picked up another Continental trick. Just over a decade ago a Swiss doctor named Fick invented what he called a 'contact lens'—in German, of course! It was intended as a corrective device—a single piece of glass that covers the eyeball. Having tried them myself, I can assure you that they are not particularly comfortable but they are effective. To begin with the glass was plain but now he has found a way to colour it. With the result . . ."

"One can have any colour eyes one wants." Like any woman, Irene's mind had leapt to the cosmetic—as well as the criminal—possibilities.

"Yes, I'm afraid it adds one more dimension of difficulty to our beleaguered profession."

I was getting out of my depth with all this nothing-being-what-it-seemed-to-be business.

"I can't think why the fellow doesn't just change his head and have done with it," I said rather grumpily.

"As ever, old fellow, you have hit the nail on the head—though perhaps that isn't quite the expression I want!

"And now, in view of the hour, I think it would be unwise for young Ned here to be wandering the streets. I wonder, Watson, whether you would be good enough to ask Mrs. Hudson to make up the bed in the spare room? Tomorrow bids fair to be an interesting day for all of us and I commend the two of you to get a good night's sleep in readiness.

"As for me, I think there are two pipes worth of pondering between me and my bed."

My last sight of him was of a figure sunk deep within his armchair, his head so wreathed in clouds of smoke that it appeared to be disembodied.

CHAPTER TEN

"Excellent. We are travelling at fifty-three and a half miles an hour at present. We should be well on time."

Holmes took a boyish interest in trains. It was not the first time I had seen him occupy himself in this way. He would ascertain the distance between the telegraph posts along the line—in this case, sixty yards—and then consult his watch on his lap. The calculation was then, as he never tired of telling me, a simple one. I had long ceased to argue the point. We should be in Oxford soon enough.

In the opposite corner of the carriage loomed Mycroft, the sheaf of papers in his hand looking like so many playing cards. I took them to be Whitehall memoranda from the way he was shuffling and discarding them, occasionally balling one of them up with an elephantine explosion of derisive breath and dropping it into the gladstone bag that lay open at his feet. I wondered what high matter of state I was observing being born.

Finally, Holmes retrieved his watch and tapped it.

"We shall be arriving in precisely five minutes, gentlemen. Mycroft, perhaps you will be good enough to inform us of this evening's protocol. We never saw fit to have such happenings at my own *alma mater* but perhaps at The House . . . ?"

"Certainly not. We were far too serious minded. No, I am informed that the Boar's Head Banquet is a tradition that a somewhat *avant garde* Senior Common Room are *attempting* to initiate, this being their first foray. It is an attempt to integrate academia with what they euphemistically refer to as the 'real world.' To that end they invite as guests two distinguished—or, should I say, well known—figures who may be expected to take contrary positions on issues of the day. Thus creating—and please understand that I am merely quoting—'intellectual synergy.' "

"And tonight's guests just happen to be Wilde and Cain?" said Holmes thoughtfully.

"Indeed. Wilde, I gather, was invited some time ago. As I mentioned before, he was a distinguished scholar of the college in his time. The real world seems to have gone to his head . . ."

"Not to mention his mouth," I heard myself say. Both heads turned as one in my direction.

"*Touché*, Doctor," said Mycroft.

"Still, it would never do to underestimate Mr. Wilde. *He* certainly never does. As for Cain, I gather he offered his services some few weeks ago and, in the light of the public attention he is currently attracting . . ."

"We are to be given rooms in college overnight

and the banquet is to be preceded by a reception in the Master's Lodge at which both men will be asked to speak—hopefully, briefly. We then go into the Hall for the meal. Lestrade has his men deployed around the college grounds. If they are as successful tonight as on the two previous occasions, they will probably succeed in arresting one of the Magdalen deer! Personally, I could never feel comfortable in an institution that encourages wildlife to wander around the place."

I have always found it strangely childish the way the rivalry between the different colleges persists into adult life. It's exactly the same, whether it's Oxford or Cambridge. My own family circumstances had never permitted my going to either, so I can be reasonably objective, I hope, and frankly, I found Magdalen College on this, my first visit, to be magnificent.

Mycroft, to do him justice, realising my interest, instructed the driver at the station to take a detour, so that we could approach it from the river side. Even though dusk had fallen, the tower was a splendid sight against the evening sky and I could well imagine May Morning with the choristers welcoming the dawn and the students—most of whom had stayed up all night for that very same purpose—crowded in punts on the water below. The bells were still ringing in my ears, so to speak, as we descended from the cab at the college gates.

As the porters unloaded our luggage from the cab, I noticed that Holmes insisted on taking one bag into his personal care. It resembled nothing so much as a large hat box and I had noticed that he had stowed it with great care on the luggage rack in the train. When I had remarked that he seemed to be bringing a great deal for such a short stay, he brushed me aside with—"Watson, don't you worry your head about that"—or some such reply.

Now the Bursar—an old friend of Mycroft's, it appeared—hurried up to welcome us and soon we were walking though the ancient grounds. Movement in the far distance caught my eye and I guessed they were the deer for which Magdalen is famous.

"Wildlife!" Mycroft hissed in my ear.

Once settled in our rooms in the main quadrangle, we had time for a leisurely bath before changing and being escorted by one of the junior dons to the Master's Lodge.

The air was crisp and the moon bright, casting dramatic shadows over centuries' old stonework and glass. At a moment like this I could quite see the timeless attraction of the scholar's life, so different from the disorderly affairs that occupied the world outside its walls.

We were among the last to arrive and the

elegantly-appointed room was crowded. All our hosts, naturally, were wearing their academic dress—long black gowns draped with various colourful "collars" denoting their status. The rest of us were, as requested, in evening dress.

Formal dress, I have to admit, does little for me, except make me feel vaguely uncomfortable but it transforms Holmes. The black makes that lean figure look even taller and more impressive. Or perhaps he regards it as one more disguise and thinks himself into the part. How does one tell when an actor is acting?

I now had an opportunity to study the Master, Cyril Overton. A small, gnome-like man but a brilliant one in his own field, Mycroft had informed us. He had been writing his great work on Byzantium for at least forty years.

"Well, the place has waited long enough. I don't suppose another few years will make too much difference," I'd said but the levity seemed to go unappreciated.

Now Overton was buzzing around from group to group, as if seeking to pollinate them with whatever was on his mind. When he came to temporary rest next to us, it was clear that the subject was the Boar's Head Banquet.

"So many of our contemporaries are hopelessly mired in the past," he enthused. "And while, naturally, I yield to no one in my admiration for the glories of antiquity, we must also move with the times. I envision in the years, as they unfold, a roll call of the great and good . . ."

His eyes flickered to where Janus Cain and his sombre entourage were the centre of a chattering group.

". . . and the indubitably interesting. And if my own poor contribution to this bold new tradition should happen to be recalled in some footnote . . ."

"What is the significance of the Boar's Head?" I asked. Over the Master's head I could see an impassive Mycroft mouthing the word "Wildlife."

"Ah, now there I *can* claim a modicum of credit," Overton enthused. "The serving of the boar's head is normally associated with Christmas. As I'm sure you know, the custom derives from Norse mythology. Freyr, the god of peace and plenty, used to ride on the boar, Gullinbursti. At his festival the head of the boar was ceremoniously served to the gathering and a traditional carol sung. A picturesque concept, to be sure. But *my* concept was to adapt the ceremony to celebrate the peace and plenty of *ideas,* do you see? And, of course, the boar is a wild one hunted on our own estate. I shall be most interested to hear your views at the end of the evening, Mr. Holmes. And now, gentlemen, if you will excuse me . . . ?"

He buzzed away and soon we could hear him

saying to the next group . . . "Now there I *can* claim a modicum of credit . . ."

At that moment Oscar Wilde made his entrance. I use the word advisedly, for he posed in the doorway until everyone in the room was aware of his presence.

He was dressed in red velvet from head to foot and wore a soft Renaissance style hat, which he now doffed as he gave a low, sweeping bow to the assembled gathering. When he was assured of their attention, he said—

"It is always nice to be expected and not to arrive. But then, while I could deny myself the pleasure of talking, I could not deny to others the pleasure of listening."

The next moment he was in the midst of the crowd, greeting everyone as an old friend and acting as though we had all been invited to *his* party, which, in a way, we had.

I looked across at Cain. It was obvious that he was not well pleased to have the attention taken away from him as completely as this and it was certainly not what he had become used to lately.

I turned to say as much to Holmes and Mycroft, only to find them engaged in one of their typically elliptical conversations. In this case they were discussing Wilde . . .

"Insecure . . ."

"Frightened, even . . ."

"Feet . . ."

"The Law . . ."

"Certainly. Angry . . ."

"Now, come, gentlemen," I said, "I know you like to play your little games for my bewildered benefit but will you please explain . . ."

Holmes sighed. "Mr. Wilde is insecure today, as is evidenced by the fact that he has tied his brand new cravat several times before getting it to his satisfaction. The alternative creases are quite evident . . ."

"As is the fact that he was careless with his shoes. The left is laced differently from the right—something a man of his fastidious manners would never normally permit . . ." Mycroft added.

"And when one adds the fact that in shaving he has missed a small area at the corner of his mouth, the case for his lack of concentration is, I believe, complete."

"And the Law? And his being angry?" I interposed.

Holmes continued, as though it were all perfectly obvious.

"The paper—which has clearly, by its crumpled appearance, been thrust into his coat pocket—has the unmistakable look of a legal document. I would guess that its contents have so angered him that he straightway dashed off a reply. The ink on his fingers is clearly of recent origin and he does not strike me as a man who is normally in any way careless of his personal appearance, particularly when appearing in public. *Ergo*, he is involved in a legal matter of some urgent concern to him . . .

"Unless, of course, he has just dashed off another comedy. You of all people know what these writer fellows are, Doctor? I believe he has another one opening in a day or two, has he not?"

There was the tapping of a fork on a glass and Overton called for attention. In a speech as carefully wrought as any of his classical texts he explained the *raison d'être* of the banquet—a story almost everyone in the room must have heard already in some detail.

He then called upon his guests to grace our gathering with a few words. Just as he had introduced Cain, a college servant entered and plucked urgently at his sleeve. Apologising profusely, the Master left the room. For some reason this seemed to disconcert Cain, at whom I happened to be looking at the time. He murmured something to one of his acolytes, who also slipped unobtrusively away.

Cain began to speak and it was fascinating the way he delivered essentially the same message but managed to tailor it to the susceptibilities of his audience. Instead of fire and brimstone, it was ironic intellectual speculation, liberally laced with literate quotations drawn from what I assumed to be the accepted texts of comparative religion. His audience responded to his performance as they would to that of a skilled actor.

I turned to say as much to Holmes, only to find that he was no longer at my side. Nor, as far as I could determine, was he anywhere in the room.

Cain was now moving into his peroration. Interestingly, he was no longer claiming to be God's personal appointee for the wrath to come but the message was the same.

The Apocalypse was upon us and the sound we could hear was that of the hooves of the First Horseman—Pestilence. Any moment now he would be in our midst. On that sombre note he ended.

Now it was Wilde's turn.

And the man was amazing. Gone was the gadfly of the Café Royal. Among his intellectual equals he was on his mettle. And how he spoke. The voice was not loud but he played it like a cello, soft and liquid. He took ideas and played with them, tossing them up in the air, then discarding them.

He picked up where Cain had left off and teased religion. While he admired those who could quote from the Bible at such length and possess the gift of tongues, was it not incredibly painful to speak in perpetual italics?

He envied people who had religion, he really did. Unfortunately, he did not think he had one himself—he was an Irish Protestant . . . People were always worrying that their sins would find them out. "But it is when they find you *in* that trouble begins." As for prayer—"Prayer must never be answered. If it is, it ceases to be prayer and becomes correspondence." His own relationship with God he found to be a little sad. "One half of the world does not believe in God, and the other half does not believe in me." In fact, he sometimes thought that God, in creating Man, somewhat over-estimated his ability . . .

He turned his attention to Academia . . .

"Education is an admirable thing," he said seriously, scanning the room, "but it is well to remember from time to time that nothing that is worth knowing can be taught . . . Examinations are of no value whatsoever. If a man is a gentleman, he knows quite enough, and if he is not a gentleman, whatever he knows is bad for him.

"The whole theory of modern education is radically unsound. Fortunately, in England, at any rate, education produces no effect whatsoever. If it did, it would prove a serious danger to the upper classes, and probably lead to acts of violence in Grosvenor Square." Then, more seriously, "We teach people how to remember, we never teach them how to grow."

What did he think of Cambridge? Someone shouted out.

"It is the best preparatory school for Oxford that I know."

And Oxford?

"The capital of romance—in its own way as memorable as ancient Athens. People say it is the home of impossible ideals and lost causes; for myself, I think that some of those causes have simply been temporarily mislaid . . ."

And finally he came back to this evening. He was touched that his old college had been so influenced by his as yet unproduced masterpiece, *Salomé*, that they should adopt the theme for their inaugural banquet but he sincerely hoped that they had taken care to exchange the head of the Magdalen Boar for that other Baptist bore, sometimes known as John!

He touched precisely the right note for the gathering—playful but informed. Behind me I heard someone whisper—"They say he was the best talker Oxford ever heard"—and his companion reply—"Probably the best talker *anyone* has ever heard."

Wilde's hearing must have been unusually acute for he heard them. "Ah, if only someone would teach the English how to talk and the Irish how to listen, what a world we should have . . ."

Now the Bursar—in the Master's absence—was asking us to move over to the Hall, where the banquet was about to be served. As the other guests began drifting out, I looked questioningly at Mycroft but it was obvious that he was as puzzled by Holmes's disappearing act as I was. The room continued to thin until we had no alternative but to leave in our turn and hurry through the chill night air towards the beckoning lights of the Great Hall.

If you live in a place it is inevitable that you eventually take it for granted but to me the room we entered was a revelation. High and vaulted with its ancient blackened beams, it spoke of generations of students, many of whom had shaped the world they inherited. Here they had sat down the centuries, just as we sat now, staring at the paintings of anonymous forebears and speculating on their lives and fortunes. This was part of the tradition Holmes and I—in our small way—were dedicated to defend.

At dinner the two empty places on the High Table were as visible as missing teeth. In his opening remarks of welcome, the Bursar did his elegant best to excuse the Master's absence. To which Wilde was heard to remark in a stage whisper—with a sidelong glance at Cain—that presumably the call of the Almighty outranked even that of the Master.

It was clear, however, that the role of under-study was not one that the Bursar had either expected or enjoyed and he was obviously relieved when the first course had been cleared away and he could announce the evening's *pièce de résistance.*

"As you heard the Master say earlier, we very much hope that this evening will come to be a permanent date on all our calendars, a symbolic *coup de grâce* of the mind, as it were, a *fons et origo*, a . . ." and here his linguistic allusions seemed to desert him. He hurried on . . .

"So, gentlemen, may I ask you to charge your glasses and be upstanding, as we sing the traditional hymn, originally sung before Prince Henry at St. John's College at Christmas 1607."

As he spoke, the College choir in full regalia had quietly assembled behind us and now began to sing *a cappella* . . .

> The Boar is dead
> So, here is his head;
> What man can have done more
> Than his head off to strike,
> Meleager like
> And bring it as I do before?

As the final notes died away, the Bursar raised his glass—"The Boar's Head!"

We all solemnly echoed him—"The Boar's Head!"—and, assuming that was what was intended, resumed our seats in a rather uncoordinated fashion. As we did so, there was a flourish of trumpets—that reminded me uncomfortably of the previous evening at Cain's rally—and the great doors swung open to reveal the Head Chef and his retinue of underlings.

In his arms he bore a gigantic covered salver. In stately fashion the procession walked around the perimeter of the hall and approached the top table. Reverently, the salver was presented to the Bursar, who bowed. The Chef bowed in reply, then set it before the Bursar in a space that had been conveniently cleared. There followed an expectant and dramatic pause. Then the Chef with a practised flourish, whisked away the cover—to reveal . . .

. . . a boar's head, smiling cheerfully with an apple in its mouth . . .

. . . and the head of Sherlock Holmes!

CHAPTER ELEVEN

If a hundred people can gasp in unison, then that was the sound that reverberated around that hall. The Artful Dodger could have picked every pocket in the place without the slightest difficulty, for every eye was on that platter.

The boar's head sat there with that air of slight surprise that has distinguished boars' heads through the ages. And next to it, examining it quizzically, was Holmes. It was the stuff of nightmares.

I found myself gripping Mycroft's sleeve as if I would never let it go. And then behind us, from the back of the hall, I heard a voice say—

"Gentlemen, I do hope you will excuse this somewhat excessive touch of theatricality. I confess that our two guest speakers touched off my competitive instincts and I felt compelled to make a statement of my own on this hallowed occasion. Consider it, if you will, a piece of living—or, perhaps I should more accurately say, dead—art. Drawn from a Biblical quotation— Proverbs, I believe—I call it—'Two Heads Are Better Than One.'"

And Sherlock Holmes walked in dead silence to take up his place on the High Table, as if it were the most natural thing in the world.

Then, as the decibel level rose all around the room, he reached across me and handed an envelope each to the Bursar and Janus Cain.

The Bursar, I thought, looked positively relieved to read his. In fact, he rose to his feet immediately and rapped the table for silence.

"Gentlemen, I have a message here from the Master. He regrets that he can not be with us on his historic evening but he has been summoned personally by the Prime Minister himself on an urgent mission of national importance."

There was a ripple of speculation around the room. And then I glanced at Cain.

His expression started as surprise, then melted successively through shock and anger into a frozen malevolence that had but one focus—the man sitting next to me, who appeared completely oblivious.

Slowly the noise level returned to normal, the offending platter was removed and centuries of tradition reasserted themselves. The dinner was resumed, the inevitable speeches followed and the evening wound to its preordained close.

After a suitable period of socialising, the three of us found ourselves in Mycroft's rooms overlooking the main quadrangle. The full moon picked out small groups of people strolling to their respective quarters. Since the evening's food and drink had been every bit as copious as I had been led to expect from the Magdalen kitchens, it seemed to me that few of them were feeling the cold night air.

When everything is in motion, the stationary object stands out in stark relief. The cheerful homegoers were like eddies swirling around a black rock formed by three people standing in earnest conversation. Even from here I could identify Cain, Sugarman and another of his henchmen and it was clear that, whatever Cain was saying to them, it was making them extremely uncomfortable. Finally, he seemed to dismiss them and they slouched away like two whipped curs.

Cain stood there and one could feel the tension in his tall frame. By now he was alone in the quadrangle—or so he believed. Suddenly, he rushed up to a nearby tree. To my eye it looked like an ancient mulberry that had presumably survived the floods, fires and intellectual anguish of centuries. Taking one of its bare branches in both hands, he ripped it from the trunk and hurled it from him. It was an obscene and brutal act that made me shiver to watch it.

As I turned away from the window, it was apparent to me that both Holmes and Mycroft had witnessed the very same incident.

"The abyss looms, I fancy," said Mycroft. "And now, Sherlock. A word of explanation, if you please . . ."

Holmes, I thought, looked like a small boy

who has just played a trick on grownups and is defiantly pleased with himself.

"It seemed to me that it was high time Mr. Cain was pulled up short. He had been having things his own way for too long. First Lady Hatton, then the judge—and the taunting little notes. To say nothing of his hounding of Miss Adler . . ."

What, I asked myself, was the *real* order of priority here?

"With rare exceptions the criminal mind is inclined to create its own tracks and then run on them. Most criminals are caught because they repeat themselves. Cain—for I find it less confusing to use his new name—likes to pun and create identities for people, not merely himself.

" 'Fallen Woman' . . . 'Hanging Judge' . . . So what might we have in mind for the Master of an Oxford college on the occasion of an event the victim himself has christened—somewhat fancifully—The Boar's Head Banquet? 'College Head,' perhaps? It seemed a reasonable deduction that it would have something to do with decapitation—which also happens to be his preferred form of retribution . . ."

"So you decided on the pre-emptive strike, so to speak?" said Mycroft.

"And enlisted the aid of Monsieur Oscar Meunier of Grenoble . . ." I added. "A name I have good reason to remember . . ."

"Indeed, you do, Watson, indeed you do."

164

Holmes rubbed those long thin hands of his together in boyish relish.

"You will recall, Mycroft, that when I returned to London last year after the little hiatus caused by Moriarty, I was literally drawing the fire of his sole remaining aide, the infamous Colonel Sebastian Moran . . ."

" 'The second most dangerous man in London,' I believe you dubbed him?"

"By this time the *most* dangerous—at least, as far as I was concerned. I ascertained that he intended to assassinate me by shooting me with a patent air rifle from the window of the unoccupied house opposite . . ."

"I called the story 'The Empty House,' " I said proudly.

"One of your very finest, Doctor," Mycroft nodded magisterially. "I declare I could quote it to you almost word for word."

"Yes, yes, I must admit you curbed some of your more romantic flourishes for once." Holmes was never best pleased when the attention was distracted from him in full flow.

"In which case you will recall how I lured Moran to fire at what was, in reality, a wax effigy of me which I had placed in the window of 221B. You can still see the bullet mark just under the angle of the chin . . . And so I determined that if the work of Mr. Meunier could deceive the eagle eye of the then most dangerous man in London, it

165

had every chance of doing the same for Mr. Janus Cain—especially when what he was expecting to see on that silver salver was the head of that celebrated classicist, Cyril Overton . . ."

Seeing that both Mycroft and myself were opening our mouths in unison, Holmes rushed on, rather than risk interruption . . .

"It was obvious to me that Cain was not committing these recent crimes unaided. Oh, he may very well have administered the *coup de grâce* to keep his hand in, so to speak, for old times' sake, but there was no way he could have strung up the Judge from the rigging single-handed. And it seemed to me extremely unlikely that he would chance his arm—if I may mix a metaphor—in front of this evening's gathering.

"No, Cain's 'faithful' were charged with that task. While Cain was speaking in full view of all of us, Overton was to have been lured out of the room and 'prepared' for the banquet . . ."

"But the Master *was* called away and no one has seen him since . . ."

"Yes, but by me. A little high handed on my part, I am afraid. When Overton left the room, he was met by Lestrade and escorted to special transport that is even now carrying him to London, where he believes he is to have a private audience with the Prime Minister. A slight exaggeration on my part, I fear. In reality, he will be seen by one of the Prime Minister's closest confidants, where

166

the gravity of the situation will be explained to him in general terms. He will then be escorted to a safe residence for the duration 'in the national interest.' There will be some reference made to a possible honour in the Queen's Birthday List. The country cannot afford to imperil such a towering talent. That sort of thing . . . As far as Cain is concerned, Overton is one pawn that is no longer on the board to be taken . . ."

"And that, I presume, was the content of the note delivered to Cain at dinner?" Mycroft enquired.

"In a sense. I also enclosed a copy of the entry from tomorrow's agony column that Cain had placed. The quotation from Proverbs about two heads being better than one. I added a copy of the entry that *I* had placed adjacent to it . . ."

"Which read . . . ?"

"Which read—

'THERE SHALL NO RAZOR
COME UPON HIS HEAD'
(Numbers 6:5)

"But perhaps the most significant event of the entire evening was the one we just witnessed . . ."

"In what sense, Holmes?"

"The man is beginning to come apart. The gears are clashing instead of meshing. He has become so convinced of his innate superiority that he

167

cannot deal with a situation in which he is not in complete control.

"The game of personal revenge is now over and the outcome is less than satisfactory to him. Yet this is a man who must act . . ."

Mycroft mused aloud . . .

> "And enterprises of great pith and
>   moment
> With this regard their currents turn awry,
> And lose the name of action.

"Hamlet—as usual—was quite right. I'm sorry, Sherlock, I did not mean to interrupt."

"I'm afraid, gentlemen," Holmes continued, "that I have deliberately precipitated the next phase—whatever that may be. Cain will now seek to accelerate his master plan. And we must find out what that plan is before it is too late."

Then, as if on cue, there came a soft tap at the door.

"Come," boomed Mycroft, the setting seemingly taking him back to imperious student days.

Around the door appeared the tentative head of Oscar Wilde.

"I have no wish to intrude, as I see you have sported your oak . . ." he said in a surprisingly normal tone.

"Closing the outer door for privacy," Holmes explained for my benefit.

And then Wilde seemed to pick up the earlier thought.

"What is it about this place that makes one revert to habits and speech patterns one had long since thought to have given up?"

Then, more like his usual self . . .

"My dear Holmes—if I may be allowed the intimacy—I simply came to say how relieved I am to see that you have kept your head under these trying circumstances. No, perhaps that is not precisely true. I rarely say anything simply.

"I also bring news of our mutual friend. Whether they are 'clues,' as you professionals call them, I leave to you to decide."

"Pray continue, Mr. Wilde. After this evening, I would find your insights most instructive," said Holmes but in a tone I had rarely heard him employ. I had the distinct impression that he was beginning to take a more positive view of this unusual man.

"We happen to have been allocated adjacent rooms and I was attempting to collect my thoughts—as well as the far more difficult task of choosing my cravat—before attending our little *soirée*. I just happened to have my door ajar the merest crack . . ."

I wonder why? I thought.

". . . and three of the most loathsome men kept coming to and fro, as if on errands for Mr. Cain. Their appearance and demeanour was utterly unaesthetic. I really don't know what the college is coming to.

"To begin with, Cain seemed quite cheerful. In fact, he kept whistling that rather repetitive little French tune. Yes, that's the one—but how . . . ?"

Holmes had whistled the fateful six notes, as if anticipating what our guest was going to say.

"Ah, well, you have your methods, I'm sure. But as the visits continued, it became clear that, whatever their mission, these men were not succeeding to his satisfaction. Voices became raised . . ."

"I made sure Overton was never left alone," Holmes said to Mycroft and myself in a voice so soft that Wilde did not even pause in his narrative.

". . . and by the time he left, Cain was a very angry man. I saw his face as he passed my door and his florid complexion gave me a distinct recollection of the dear Marquess of Queensberry—but that is another story. I waited for a while, naturally. After all, no *diva* makes an entrance until the supporting players are already on stage to create a context. And then . . ."

"Yes?" Now Holmes seemed genuinely interested. It was as though what Wilde had reported so far merely confirmed what he already knew.

"Then—we left the hall together just now after your own little *divertissement* and I was chatting to him in my usual charming fashion, although

I must admit he had little to contribute—except *one* thing . . .

"I happened to mention that I have my new play opening in a few days' time on February 14th. It is, frankly, my *chef d'oeuvre* to date. I insist that you all come to the opening night. The play is quite brilliant. I call it a trivial comedy for serious people. All that remains is to see whether the audience is worthy of it. I said—I thought charmingly—that it would be my personal Valentine to my public. And then *Cain* said . . ."

"Try and remember the precise words he used," Holmes said urgently.

Wilde thought for a moment. Then—

"Cain said that was interesting. 'Then there will now be *two* presents on Valentine's Day. For I have one for the whole of London.' "

CHAPTER TWELVE

By mid-morning we were back in Baker Street with a great deal on our minds. In the train we were each wrapped in our respective mantles of silence.

We knew our adversary. We also knew that the events of the previous evening had put a match to the blue touch paper that was Cain. But what kind of explosion could we expect and where would it occur?

Mycroft returned to the labyrinths of Whitehall, where he would ensure the continued absence of Cyril Overton for the duration—even though I strongly suspected that he had now been dismissed from Cain's stage as an irrelevant "extra."

Strangely, Holmes's first priority, once we had unpacked, seemed to be the cleaning of his own waxen image. I was reminded of Hamlet fussing with Yorick's skull as he carefully wiped and polished it, muttering to himself—"Congealed gravy! Meunier would never forgive me . . ."

The whole spectacle was so bizarre that I soon left to attend to a number of business matters around town. Exciting as it often is to be involved in Holmes's escapades, it does play havoc with the minutiae of day to day life. What with one thing and another—a visit to the club being the other—it was well after the noon hour before I returned to our rooms.

As I entered, I found Holmes curled up in his favourite chair like a cat and smoking his old clay pipe. Judging from the texture of the air around his head he had been there ever since I went out. That in itself was not unusual but the expression on his face was.

"Watson," he said, without even looking in my direction, "I have just had a visitation."

"Oh," I replied facetiously, "you mean like *A Christmas Carol*? The Ghost of Holmes Past? Probably to do with polishing that stupid head . . ."

Then I saw that my attempt at humour was inappropriate. Something had seriously discomposed my friend. Fortunately, he did not appear to have heard me.

"I can think of only one other comparable occasion and that was the time Professor Moriarty visited me and threatened my life—with the result you know.

"This morning, soon after you had gone—in fact, he must have waited until he had seen you go—Janus Cain came here.

"Mrs. Hudson was also out doing her morning shopping and no one rang the bell—but the next thing I knew, he was here in the room."

"Good heavens, Holmes! The man might have murdered you!"

"Oh, there was little fear of that, old fellow. These days I am a lot less trusting of *homo sapiens*. Or *femina sapiens*—if such a species exists. You will have observed that I keep my loaded stick near to hand and there is a handy revolver tucked under this cushion at all times. No, Cain was not here to kill me—merely to *warn* me . . ."

"Warn you of what?"

"Warn me that I had meddled with the ways of the Lord—*his* Lord. 'And my God is a jealous God, Mr. Holmes,' he said. 'He brooks no interference but strikes down all who stand in His Path and defy His Purpose . . .'

"Then he grew a little confused and it was not clear whether he was doing the talking or whether his 'God' was supposed to be talking though him. His identity seemed to come and go.

"We have been conscious of your presence for some time . . . In a previous life you caused us grave inconvenience and interfered with the holy work we were sent to do here. It was you who caused us to be banished into the wilderness. There we wandered and all men set their hand against us . . ."

"If the man is serious, he's certifiable, Holmes."

". . . and now you are playing the busybody all over again—you and that gross brother of yours and that oafish doctor friend . . ."

For once I was speechless. "Oafish," indeed!

Holmes caught my eye for the first time.

"Don't concern yourself unduly, old friend. He had much worse to say about me. And by this time it was clear that Daintry was firmly back in control, at least for the moment. It was like listening to two or three different people inhabiting the same body. Quite unnerving, I can assure you. A moment or two later Cain had returned . . .

"But the Lord found me. He came to me as an epiphany in a vision on the mountain top. He raised me and bathed my wounds. He entered my soul and transformed me to what you see now. He imbued me with His Purpose—and I shall fulfill that Purpose. None of your puny efforts shall stand in my way.

"I am here today, Sherlock Holmes to serve you notice. You have ensured that God's vengeance will be even more terrible than was first intended . . .

"By this time the man—Cain, Daintry, whoever he was—was striding around the room. Oh, I kept a careful eye on him," Holmes quickly added, sensing my concern, "but I no longer felt I was in immediate danger. He had come to pour out his bile. In a strange way I actually felt quite sorry for him. Whatever was causing it, he was in genuine pain. I must admit to you, Watson, that my own thoughts were more than a little confused by now but I knew that it was my one chance to draw information from him while he was in this mood."

"And precisely what form may we expect this Divine Retribution to take?" I asked.

"It was the wrong question, old friend, the wrong question. For it triggered some safety mechanism in that distorted brain. It was the cunning old Daintry who looked back at me, even though he answered in the voice of Cain.

"Remember the Apocalypse, Mr. Holmes. The Four Horsemen . . .

"Yes, Pestilence . . . Famine . . . War . . . and Death, if I recall?

"Correct. And the First Horseman shall be Pestilence . . . 'I will smite them with pestilence and disinherit them.' Book of Numbers. Chapter Fourteen, Verse Twelve. Study it well, Mr. Holmes, for it may be the last book you ever read . . .

"And with that, Watson, he was at the door. 'Pestilence shall lead the way but the rest will surely follow. And then I shall create the Lord's new dominion here on earth.'

"He clearly intended this to be his grand exit but I'm afraid I rather—what do the actors say?—I rather 'trod on his lines.' As he was turning to go, I said . . . 'A plague on *all our houses, eh?* Sometimes I find the Bard more apposite than the Book. And one other thing—it may well be that *your* Numbers and *my* numbers add up

176

to a different total, Mr. Cain. Had your ego not intervened and led you to pay off old scores, I might never have become involved in your new devilry. But once I knew the Ripper was back, I had scores of my own to settle.

" 'But you talk of your *new* vision. May I ask you a question, Mr. Cain? How can your plan be completed until you have found Senta or Violetta or—*Irene?*'

"He slammed the door so hard we may need to have someone look at the hinges."

Now, for the first time since he had begun his narrative, he rose to his feet and strode over to the bay window. I went to his side and stood at his shoulder, as he looked down into the street below. To my eye it looked no different from any other day with the clip-clop of the hansoms and the ever-moving skein of people going about their business but Holmes obviously saw something more.

"To men like Cain—or Moriarty in his day— the individual is meaningless, yet each of those little dots is a human life. Each has its hopes and fears and dreams and deserves the right to play out the hand that God has dealt it. None of us has the right to usurp that role and play God.

"I have never felt more sure in my life, old fellow, than I did just now that we stand poised to help millions of our fellow men and women— or fall into the pit along with them.

"Come along, Watson, we haven't a moment to lose . . ."

"Where are we going to, Holmes?"

"To lunch at a certain club in St. James's, Watson, where I happen to know the kitchen closes early. Even in times of crisis it does not do to ignore the inner man. But I guarantee you an unusual dessert . . ."

For reasons of discretion I shall omit the name of the club. Suffice it to say that within its discreet portals many an important assignation has been made and many a decision taken that changed the course of history. From its distinctive curved windows that commanded the sweep of that distinguished thoroughfare a man might see that history unroll. But already I am in danger of giving too much away . . .

I was not aware that Holmes was a member of the club. In fact, I would have been prepared to bet that he was not but Mycroft's influence and the high regard in which he himself was held ensured that this was not a problem. He was greeted with understated effusiveness and we were shown to a table in a quiet corner, where we could talk without being overheard.

Over lunch we reviewed what we knew of Cain's recent history and it was frustratingly little and irritatingly contradictory.

"The man has gone to great pains to make

himself into an instant celebrity on the public stage. There can be scarcely a person in London, at least, who does not know of him. He preaches Doom and they shudder deliciously, as though he were reading them a tale by the Brothers Grimm. He is the Chief Barker at some religious carnival . . ."

Holmes traced the tines of his fork on the linen table cloth, creating a grooved pattern of tighter and tighter circles that seemed to represent our progress.

". . . and yet all of this is a snare and delusion. People are lulled into believing that he is an entertainer when, in reality, we have reason to know that he means every word. What we still do not know is how he means to achieve it, how he means to bring about his version of the Apocalypse.

"There are two men in London who may be able to help us in this regard. Let us take our coffee and consult one of them . . ."

As we descended the stairs, Holmes sketched in a brief background of the man we were about to meet.

"Langdale Pike is a human book of reference on scandal. London is his web and this club is the epicentre of it. All gossip reverberates through his strands. Some of it he turns into lucrative little paragraphs for those periodicals that cater to a prurient public. The rest he peddles in a variety of other ways. I freely confess, old fellow, that I have, from time to time, had cause to use his services myself and have, on occasion, even helped him in turn. I do not, I should add, regard those as among my finest hours. Ah, here we are . . ."

We had reached one of the club's sitting rooms that faced on to the street. It was empty except for the effete and languid creature who sat in the bow of the window like some well-worn advertisement, there to see and be seen by all who passed by.

He was extremely thin and appeared to be tall, although he never once rose from his seated position during the whole time we were there. Hair and complexion were of a uniform washed out grey and in the bony face his nose—as Shakespeare says of Falstaff—was "as sharp as a pen." But it was the eyes that drew your attention. I don't know if eyes can be "flat" but his were— flat and restless. They flickered over us and back to the window. You knew they missed nothing.

If he was surprised to see Holmes unannounced, he displayed no sign of it. Perhaps the extra beat of attention he paid to me represented some form of enquiry, for it prompted my friend to introduce us. Pike did not offer his hand and I certainly did not seek it. I sensed that it would resemble the skin texture of the ugly fish that shared his name.

"Janus Cain," said Holmes to the averted head at the window.

"Ah, I was wondering who would be the first . . ." And for the next ten minutes this odd little man—for, despite his height, he seemed curled up on himself—recited chapter and verse as though he were reading it out of a book of reference. He clearly possessed a remarkable and retentive memory, for there was much in what he said that was missing from Holmes's Index entry.

Unfortunately, among all the detail surrounding Cain's appearances, there was little that added to our knowledge of his underlying purpose. As if sensing our frustration, it was as though Pike turned to a new chapter.

"Before Cain arrived in London, there was a sudden movement in the property market—in Whitechapel, of all places. A series of houses—workmen's cottages—were bought up. The whole of two streets, in fact, and a square in between. The supposition was that someone had purchased cheap property for the land it stood on and that someone would demolish the existing structures to build something of style and substance. In the event no such thing happened. Oh, there was building work done, right enough, but not by locals—which caused its own antipathy. The workmen were shipped in from the Continent and shipped out again when the work was done. Rumour has it that the whole interior was gutted and totally transformed—into what nobody can say, although there was talk of quantities of laboratory equipment being unloaded at dead of night.

"The fact of the matter is that no one has seen inside the new structure. One morning, when the locals awoke from their gin-ridden slumbers . . ." —and here Pike took a sip from what looked suspiciously like a tumbler of gin—"they found themselves looking at The Church of the New Apocalypse . . . and Mr. Janus Cain *(sic)* was in residence."

"The money?" Holmes asked.

"Now that *is* an interesting aspect." Pike very nearly smiled at the mention of a subject that was clearly dear to his heart. "Mr. Cain makes a repetitive point of not accepting donations from his *soi-disant* parishioners. 'It is more blessed to give than to receive,' I believe he is fond of saying. Nor, as far as I have been able to ascertain, does he have local backers. With his present, shall we say—eminence, those members of our gilded society who had put their money in Cain's purse could never resist the opportunity to boast of it. Ah, 'the pomp and vanity of this wicked world,' as he himself might say—had the Book of Common Prayer not said it first.

"However, my friends in Lombard Street do speak—admittedly, in hushed tones—of large sums being transferred across that divisive stretch of water that cuts the Continent off from civilisation as we know it. Mr. Cain, in short, has a paymaster of seemingly infinite resource. He is, perhaps, not the Puppet Master so much as a rather large puppet himself. Why, in the golden age of our mutual acquaintance . . ."

But before he could complete the thought, Holmes had risen to his feet and cut him off. As I rose to join him . . .

"Pike, you are—as always—a treasure trove . . . or do I mean trough? . . . of information. And speaking of treasure, you will, I know, give me an accounting in due course?"

"You may rest your reputation on it, my dear Mr. Holmes."

And for another brief moment the eyes were turned in our direction. As we left the club and passed the window, I could see that he was writing something in a small notebook with a thin gold pencil and he was managing to do so without taking his eyes off the road.

"You must allow me my little secrets, Watson. The air of omniscience it pleases me to create is a compound of many things and many people. Pike is one of them. He is—like Autolycus in *The Winter's Tale*—'a snapper-up of unconsidered trifles' but many of them are not trifling in my eyes or for my purposes.

"The man we are about to meet—though not

to see—is another such. In all the years we have done business together I have never set eyes on him. He chooses to call himself 'Fred Porlock' but that is no more his real name that Langdale Pike is—'Langdale Pike.' Such men swim in the shadows.

"I first encountered Porlock during that affair you were pleased to call *The Valley of Fear*. It was he who first handed me the tiny thread that finally unravelled the Moriarty organisation. 'Porlock' himself was a supernumerary in that organisation but, unlike the rest, he somehow retained a flicker of conscience—a flicker I managed to fan into an occasional flame by the use of a judicious ten pound note. He would once or twice give me advance information, which was of inestimable value—that highest value which anticipates and prevents rather than avenges crime. I live in hopes that he will do so again today.

"Since Moriarty's demise he has been operating as a freelance of sorts, though something about his response to my note suggests to me that he may once again have taken the Devil's shilling."

"Langdale Pike I can understand as a choice of name," I said. We were now bowling along in a cab towards an address in Lambeth. "It has an aristocratic ring to it and I presume 'Pike'— whoever he may be in reality—comes from that class or he would never be able to gain access to it and its information. But 'Porlock' . . . ?"

"No doubt you remember your Coleridge, old fellow? Coleridge was dozing in his garden, when he dreamed the poem we know as 'Kubla Khan.' He awoke, tremendously excited, for he knew this would be his masterpiece. Just as he was committing it to paper, he was interrupted by the arrival of 'a person on business from Porlock.' By the time the visitor had departed, so had the rest of the poem. Our friend sees himself as an interrupter to the natural course of events—a nice irony, if you think about it."

The cab drew up in a South London side street of no particular distinction. There was the usual higgledy-piggledy combination of nondescript shops and back to back houses. Tucked among them and looking vaguely sorry for itself was a small Catholic church—St. Something-or-Other's . . . the name on the sign was too faded to read. It was a far cry from London's clubland.

Holmes read my mind, as always.

"Ours is not to reason why, old fellow. This was where I was directed to come. Perhaps we may save our souls while we are about it . . ."

So saying, he pushed open a heavy wooden door that screeched complainingly on hinges that cried out for oil. Inside the decor lived up to one's expectations. Although it was empty now, the place had a shabby, well-worn look, though not unpleasantly so. This was a place in which a family was used to meeting, a family which cared more about the purpose of the visit than impressing one another with frills and furbelows. I could imagine the many thousands over the years who had sat in those wooden pews, knelt at that rail and left feeling better than when they entered. I could not help but compare it with Cain's manufactured piety.

Holmes by now had left my side and was approaching a dark corner of the church, where I could see a confessional.

"Over here, Watson, if you please."

As I approached he pulled back the curtain and I could just about make out the grille that separated the penitent's section from that of the priest. As Holmes spoke, I thought I sensed movement in the deep shadows on the other side.

"Good evening, Mr. Porlock. This is my friend and colleague, Doctor Watson, who is good enough to help me from time to time with my investigations. We have followed your instructions to the letter. We are quite alone."

"Not a good thing to be at this precise moment, Mr. Holmes. Good day, Doctor. You are, of course, known to me. I hear of Mr. Holmes everywhere since you became his chronicler . . ."

The voice was muffled and of indeterminate age but, then, it was obvious that the man was doing his best to disguise it by changing the pitch. Then to Holmes . . .

"My present lord and master—or, should I say, the most generous of the current crop?—is not a man to be trifled with. In fact, I freely admit that he is one who makes me distinctly uncomfortable, to the point where I intend to take a little holiday . . ."

"Presumably to the West Country?"

"Oh, very good, Mr. Holmes. Doctor Watson, you will have to watch your literary laurels. But do not take Cain lightly. This man is, if anything, more dangerous than our other friend—simply because he does not care about the consequences of his actions."

"So what does he plan, Porlock?"

"I do not know for sure but it is something particularly unpleasant and I do have no intention of being around when it happens. Whatever it is, he plans it to take place . . ."

"On February the Fourteenth—two days from now."

There was a pause. "As usual, you are well informed. But you will understand that, until I have put my own plans into operation, I must protect myself. I can give you but two clues. One is my own name . . ."

"And the other?"

" 'Remember Musgrave.' And one other thing . . ."

"Yes."

"On this occasion there will be no charge. If we are spared, I hope we three shall meet again in thunder, lightning or in rain . . . who can tell?"

"Porlock?"

But there was something in the feeling of the air in that little cubicle that told one we were now alone.

CHAPTER THIRTEEN

When I came down to breakfast the next morning, the debris of two boiled eggs told me that Holmes had, for once, pre-empted my arrival. I also found that we had a visitor—a small urchin, who could and did pass for any youngster one sees anywhere on the streets of London, except for his eyes. Button bright, they missed nothing. Anyone looking into them for five seconds would have known him to be extremely wary. Fortunately for the lad and his employer—my good friend, Sherlock Holmes—no one ever did.

"Morning, Wiggins," I said.

"Mornin', Doctor," he replied, snapping to attention and giving a passable salute.

I have had cause to reflect more than once that there was an element of satire in his deference but the little charade, frankly, amuses me almost as much as it pleases him.

"What news of Irene, Holmes?"

"You'd better hear what Wiggins has to report," Holmes replied without looking up from a letter he was reading.

Wiggins permitted himself to be "at ease" and repeated what he had presumably told Holmes earlier.

"The lady wot you told me to keep an eye

189

on, she's all right for now. But, blimey, that's the strangest church I've seen in all me born days . . ."

Which doesn't give us many of either, I couldn't help thinking.

"More like a prison that anyfink else and yer never see people going in to pray, like. Not much goin' on during the day time but then at night lots of carts and drays unloading round the side. Crates and boxes and some big bottles. They're very careful wiv 'em, I can tell yer. Somefink funny's going on, if yer ask me. And all them geezers in black everywhere. Wouldn't like to meet them on a dark night . . ."

"But Miss Adler . . . ?"

"Oh, we've worked out a little code, see. She don't get out except wiv some of the uvver people what work there and once or twice wiv old Cain hisself. 'E seems to 'ave taken to 'er—I mean 'im—right enough. But every evening at five Miss Adler'll stand at one of the winders and smoke a cigarette, to show me she's all right. Last night, when she saw me across the street, she managed to slide the winder up just a touch and slipped a letter out . . ."

He looked over at Holmes, who was just finishing the last page of the letter Wiggins was obviously referring to. Without a word he passed it over to me.

The paper was rough and clearly torn from a

notebook. The writing was in pencil and appeared to have been dashed off in haste but the hand revealed was fluid and feminine and I could see the face behind the words . . .

"Dear Comrades-in-Arms . . ." it read. "Do not worry about me. I am fine for the present. This place is like a beehive. You would not believe how organised everything is—and it all revolves around Cain. Part of it deals with the Church and seems perfectly genuine, if such madness *can* be genuine. There are 'converts' like me from all over the place, sending out letters, arranging Cain's rallies. All of us live here in our own little cubicles, which I must admit are extremely comfortable, even luxurious. Money is certainly no object here!

"The worker bees buzz around happily but there is another part of the complex that we are kept well away from and which is not immediately obvious from the way the place has been built. If anyone asks, they are told that these are Mr. Cain's 'private quarters.' I have only once managed to get a quick glimpse inside when one of the aides was coming out and I could have sworn I saw some sort of laboratory but then I had to move on, as the man was becoming suspicious.

"Why does a Church need a *laboratory?* And what do all these men in black *do* when they're not guarding Cain from his admirers? I get the impression some of them are travelling around the country and perhaps setting up branches in other cities.

"Call it my woman's intuition if you like, but I *know* they are planning something terrible here. The worker bees are happy in the thought that they are safe from the wrath to come, as they put it—but I have a strong feeling no one else is.

"As far as I can make out, the 'laboratory' is in the part of the complex that used to be called Mitre Square and must have a separate entrance. I'll try and find out more.

"Your friend . . ."

"We can't leave her there, Holmes." I handed him back the letter. "Not now we know without doubt that there is villainy afoot."

Holmes's brow was deeply furrowed. He tapped the letter on his knee as he brooded on what we had just learned.

"I share your view entirely, old fellow, but if you care to look at the date on this morning's paper lying at your feet, you will note that it is February 13th . . ."

"And . . . ?"

"And Cain has promised to deliver a Valentine's Day present to the whole of London tomorrow—the *14th*. It is imperative that we discover just what that present is without delay. To remove a Trojan horse before we have sacked the city defeats the purpose of constructing it in the first place and, besides, I very much doubt if either of us is persuasive enough to convince the lady in question.

"But you are quite right. We must intensify our efforts. Yesterday—straws in the wind. Today— this. A picture is beginning to emerge, Watson— an horrendous mural painted in blood and bitterness . . ."

Then seeing that Wiggins had his eyes out on stalks, he ceased.

"Wiggins, you have, as ever, been of some small service. Pray continue to watch over Miss Adler's wellbeing, keeping your eyes ever open and your mouth firmly closed at all times. Perhaps this may assist the process."

So saying, he rose and escorted the boy to the door. I saw him palm a folded banknote into the boy's hand with the skill of a practised conjuror.

At the door Wiggins turned to give us both an angelic smile, which shone oddly through the grime, and gave a smart salute.

"Count on Wiggins, Mr. 'Olmes. Gawd bless ya, sir. And you, too, Doctor. In fact, Gawd bless us, every one."

And with that, the door closed behind him.

Holmes and I looked at one another.

"Dickens, thou shouldst be living at this hour," he smiled, as he resumed his seat.

Somehow Wiggins's performance reduced the tension we had both been feeling and we continued to analyse what we knew and what it might mean.

"We now know that Cain is well funded, that he intends to do something to disrupt the whole of London, or at least a large part of it. His total disregard for human life makes me fear the worst. In his warped mind he somehow believes that he and his immediate followers will survive what he calls the New Apocalypse . . ."

"What were the so-called 'clues' from that Porlock fellow?"

Holmes rested his head on his tented hands and looked into the far distance.

"He advised me to remember his *name*. The name 'Porlock' has no meaning, unless one relates it to Coleridge and the poem he was composing when he was interrupted—'Kubla Khan' . . .

> In Xanadu did Kubla Khan
> A stately pleasure dome decree . . ."

" '*Stately pleasure dome.*' Could that be this palace he's built in the East End?"

"Possibly, Watson, possibly. Cain certainly seems to be deriving pleasure from it. But then— 'Remember Musgrave'?"

"Well, that's obvious. One of your earliest cases—before I came on the scene. I remember your telling me all about it. 'The Musgrave

Ritual.' Some sort of nursery rhyme that told you where the lost crown of Charles I was. Or was it Charles II—I forget?"

Holmes began to recite again . . .

"Whose Was It?
His who is gone.
Who shall have it?
He who will come.
Where was the sun?
Over the oak.
Where was the shadow?
Under the elm.
How was it stepped?
North by ten, east by five and by five,
South by two and by two, west by
One and by one, and so under.
What shall we give for it?
All that is ours
Why should we give it?
For the sake of the trust.

"Two fragments written two hundred years apart that appear to have nothing in common."

"Deep waters, eh, Holmes?"

"The deepest, the very deepest . . . yet I sense something lurking in those depths . . . I wonder . . ."

And then, foolishly, I had to distract him with my next question.

"Now, why does 'Mitre Square' seem to ring a bell?"

"That question I *can* answer, old fellow. Mitre Square was the scene of one of the Ripper murders—the fourth, if I am not mistaken. Catharine Eddowes. Presumably it has some sentimental significance for our friend for him to incorporate it into his new shrine.

"The more I hear about that building, the more curious I am to see it for myself. How do you feel about a little larceny this evening, Watson?"

I have often speculated on how different things might have been if Holmes had decided to step across the other side of the line of the law. The world may have lost a great actor but it certainly lost a master criminal when he decided to prosecute crime rather than pursue it.

That evening he insisted that we dine in but instead of relying on Mrs. Hudson's good plain cooking, he arranged to have a meal sent in from Harrod's.

"A cold bird or two, old friend, a little something in aspic and a very fair bottle of Sancerre. Two more deserving fellows never lived. Tonight we drink, for tomorrow . . . who knows?" And with that somewhat qualified toast, he raised his glass.

After the table had been cleared, he began to lay out the tools of his alternative trade. Several of them I had never seen before but they certainly looked most impressive.

Seeing my expression, he demonstrated them one at a time—each a relic of a previous case.

"This jemmy dates back to the Hoxton affair . . . before your time, I fancy . . . this is the black lantern used by John Clay in 'The Red-Headed League' business. The fourth smartest man in London in his day and, when it came to daring, I would probably have put him third . . . And *this* . . ."—here he held up a bunch of picklocks—"this belonged to dear old Charlie Peace. He could have been sent down for simply *owning* them—always supposing they could have caught him. A virtuoso of the violin, Watson, and a remarkable fellow, Charlie . . ."

The light of enthusiasm was bright in his eye. "D'you know, Watson, I do believe burglary could have been an alternative profession for me, had I cared to adopt it, and I have no doubt that I should have come to the fore."

As midnight struck we sallied forth, two middle-aged burglars, dressed in dark clothing from head to foot. We had to walk a few minutes before we could hail a passing cab and then we were on our way, committed to the task ahead.

Some half an hour later the cab turned out of Fenchurch Street into Aldgate and Holmes gave the sign to stop as we reached the corner of Duke Street on the left. We waited until the cab had continued into the High Street before moving on and Holmes looked around him almost nostalgically.

"Seven years and almost nothing has changed. I swear that same set of chairs sat in that same pawnshop window and that same nightwatchman poked the same brazier in front of a hole in the road. I swore I would never return here after those fools let Daintry go free but he's back, Watson—I can smell him. And this time I mean to have him."

With that he was off, setting a good pace, despite the weight that dragged down his coat pockets. Within a short time the noise and lights of the main thoroughfare were well behind us and we had the street to ourselves, except for the occasional young boys who never seemed to sleep and flitted aimlessly from one alley to another.

And then we saw it. It wasn't that obvious at first glance but where Mitre Square had presumably been there was now a single structure. The original houses were still there but their windows had been sealed, like eyes blinded with cataracts, and a large vaulted roof linked them to the houses on the other side of the square. Walking round a second side of the square soon confirmed the impression.

That second side also revealed the front door of the Church of the New Apocalypse, signalled by a large wooden sign, carved in gothic gold letters out of a black painted background and embellished with a symbolic drawing of four horsemen, like something out of a painting by Hieronymous Bosch. Even in the dim light it was loathsomely attractive. The flickering gaslight made the riders seem to move.

My first impression was that the doorway was deserted but, as we stood in the shelter of a neighbouring house, I saw movement in the shadows opposite and the glow of two cigarettes.

"I wonder if a vengeful God approves of nicotine?" I murmured to my companion but he simply replied—"Stay here, Watson, while I reconnoitre the other side." With that he was gone as if he had never existed and I remembered someone once evincing surprise that Holmes had apparently followed him. "But I saw no one," said the poor fellow. "That is what you may expect to see when I follow you," was Holmes's rejoinder.

I continued to watch the watchers in the doorway. To judge by their monotones and their body language, they were bored by their repetitive duties and I could hardly blame them. It was late and the street was quiet. The building of this monstrosity had driven the ordinary folk of Whitechapel away. People who had trodden these shabby streets all their lives and found them home had been forced to move back and start their lives again. It was as though the life had been sucked out of the area, leaving a strange vacuum in its place.

But then, was it my imagination or were there more of those ubiquitous street urchins about than I had seen previously? There would seem to be a flicker of movement in a doorway but when I turned my head to look, it would be gone.

I was still puzzling over this when I sensed Holmes at my side once more and heard him whisper—

"If it's all the same to you, Watson, I feel the servants' entrance might be more appropriate."

Then we were making our way, keeping to the deepest shadows, around the square to what was clearly the back of the building. Here there had been no real attempt to keep up the illusion of domestic dwellings. The facades were still there but they were lined with solid brick. Set into the middle of one "side" was a loading dock of the kind one sees at commercial wharves.

"What on earth do they need that for?" I murmured. "Delivering Bibles?"

Holmes raised a finger to his lips and pointed to a steel door next to the dock. A moment later it was clear that his reconnaissance had borne fruit, for he had it open and we were inside Cain's compound with the door safely closed behind us.

The interior was lit with occasional gaslights turned low but it was enough to see that we were in some sort of man-made cavern. Overhead stretched a curved dome of a roof, though it was impossible to tell of what substance it was made. Metal pillars and struts supported it and it was clear that it spanned the whole of what had been the old Mitre Square.

Now it was a virtual city in its own right with countless doors opening off a central area in which we now stood. That area was presumably the Church itself, since it contained rows of benches grouped around what looked like a simple granite altar.

Two long floor to ceiling walls divided the space like segments of an orange. The area we were in tapered away in the distance to what must have been the public entrance we had seen earlier. To the right we could hear a subdued murmuring from what I took to be the living quarters.

"The worker bees," Holmes whispered in my ear.

The opposite wall appeared identical, until one looked closely, when it became clear that doors which superficially appeared to be wood were, in fact, made of solid steel and secured with heavy locks.

"The Ark of the New Covenant, I fancy, Watson."

All this time we had been in the shadows cast by one of the huge pillars and taking our bearings. Now it occurred to me that, successful as we had been in gaining entrance, it was nothing by comparison with the task that still lay ahead of us.

Although the Church was not by any means crowded, occasional black-suited men would wander through on some errand or other. There was no way we could hope to see what lay behind those metal doors under these circumstances.

Then I saw Holmes consult his watch and give a small smile of satisfaction. A moment later there was an explosion at the far end of the hall and black smoke began to billow into it. At the same time there began such a din of boyish voices and the clang of sticks being beaten on tin. It sounded for all the world as though a riot was erupting in the street outside. It was equally obvious that Holmes had fully expected this turn of events.

He smiled like a mischievous boy himself.

"Where would we be without The Baker Street Irregulars? Mere lads but their strength is as the strength of ten, because their hearts are pure, eh, Watson?" And then I knew why I had seen so many of them massing earlier.

"Tennyson," Holmes added. "Or close."

He then took my arm and urged me towards what looked like the main steel door. As he did so, I was aware of all the attendants rushing like so many black ants to repel what sounded like an attack on their nest.

What Holmes achieved in the next few

moments was positively frightening. I had seen him open the occasional safe before but this was different. He worked at fantastic speed producing one tool after another from the pockets of his ulster, then handling each with the strength and delicacy of the trained mechanic. It took him no more than a minute before the door was swinging silently open in his hand.

We found ourselves in a space-within-a-space. To our left, behind a padlocked grille, was a veritable arsenal.

"Why, it's enough to equip a small army," I exclaimed, as Holmes made even shorter work of the padlock.

"Which is precisely what it's *intended* to do, old fellow. These gentlemen in black are not exactly altar boys. And I'm sure it has not escaped your notice that another of the Four Horsemen of the Apocalypse is called War. We are looking at his stable. Hello, this is interesting . . ."

As he was speaking, he had picked up a brand new rifle from an open crate that contained a round dozen of them. Even though I had long since had my fill of fighting, I could not but admire its sleek lines and its well-oiled blue metal finish.

"A few of these fellows in our hands and Maiwand might have turned out very differently," I muttered and then, realising that he had spoken—"*What* is interesting?"

"These weapons—and, I suspect, most of the rest of the *matériel* in this hell hole—comes courtesy of Kaiser Wilhelm II. Yes, Watson, 'Made in Germany.' We have received word lately from several quarters that weapons like these have been infiltrated into several potential danger zones . . ." I forebore to ask who "We" were.

"The Boers in South Africa . . . the underground nationalist army that is coalescing in Ireland . . . Germany seems intent on fanning any likely flame of discontent and presumably they feel that Mr. Cain has suitable incendiary qualities. But quickly, we must see what else we have here before the Irregulars run out of steam. No, don't bother putting things back tidily—I *want* Cain to know someone was here."

We passed rapidly into another area which contained walls of shelves stacked high with provisions in cans and boxes.

"The wherewithal to feed your small army when the Horseman called Famine appears . . . And what have we here . . . ?"

We had now reached one final partition. Holmes repeated his Open Sesame performance and we found ourselves looking into a laboratory so well-equipped that it would put any London hospital to shame. Stainless steel benches gleamed dully. Rows of retorts and bunsen burners receded into the far distance. All along one wall were stacked crates and belljars full of various coloured liquids. It was clear that, during the day, the place was home to dozens of workers. But working at *what?*

"Holmes, this must be what young Wiggins saw being unloaded."

"Indeed, old fellow. And, unless I miss my guess, Pestilence is staring us in the face." His attention was rivetted by a large retort containing a singularly repulsive greenish liquid that seemed to roil and shiver in the uncertain light of our lantern. "We may just have enough time . . . Watson, would you be so good as to watch the main hall—and play *Cave* . . . ?"

With that I saw him take a pair of rubber gloves from his pocket and pick up a test tube from a nearby rack, before I hurried back to the steel door. At the end of the hall the men in black seemed to be getting matters under control. The great doors of the Church were thrown wide and the smoke was gradually dispersing. The urchins had vanished like mist in the night. It was only a matter of time before at least some of the guards returned to our end of the building.

"Holmes!" I hissed.

"Coming, Watson."

And then, in that slow motion way things always happen in dreams, we were outside the building and Holmes was reaching for his tools to relock the door. To do so he had to hand me the stoppered test tube he had been carrying so carefully.

"What is it, do you suppose?"

"I've no idea but I feel it would be most advisable to see that it stays where it is, old fellow. And now I think we have earned our rest. A profitable evening, Watson, though not inexpensive. Let me see, I offered Wiggins a sovereign a head for his merry band and unfortunately, on these occasions, Wiggins's grasp of arithmetic seems to desert him—invariably in his favour."

CHAPTER FOURTEEN

But Holmes's talk of rest turned out to be just that—talk. When I came down to breakfast the next morning, he was still engaged with his chemical apparatus that he had made a beeline for as soon as we had returned the previous evening.

His hair was disarranged, his fingers stained with chemicals and the smell in the room was indescribable. If it suggested anything, it was rotten eggs. I decided to settle for a cup of tea and some toast.

"Anything or nothing, Holmes?"

"Nothing good, Watson. It needs more qualified minds than mine but from the tests I have made I would say that this distillation, of which I took a small sample, was a hybrid enhanced to be particularly corrosive to the human digestive system and with one further disturbing property . . ."

"That sounds quite disturbing enough to me already—and what is that, pray?"

"When it comes into contact with water, the essential element multiplies manyfold. In short, water causes it to divide like a demented amoeba and become infinitely more deadly. The question is—what does he intend to do with it? And have we by our intervention—for, make no mistake, he is by now well aware of it—caused him to postpone those plans? Today, as you will recall, was the day on which he promised to surprise us . . ."

"Of course, St. Valentine's Day."

"The day on which one sends a gift—without revealing the source . . . Let us hope Lestrade brings us good news in that connection . . ."

But when the Inspector arrived a few minutes later, it was apparent from the expression on his face that he did not.

He took off his bowler hat and wiped the inner band assiduously, then dabbed at the perspiration on his forehead.

"I reckon the visitors Mr. Cain received last night—and, of course, I have no idea who *they* might have been—must have properly put the wind up him. When we got around there early this morning, following the receipt of certain information . . ."—and he cast a veiled look in Holmes's direction—"we insisted on inspecting the premises in the light of the recent fracas. That way it doesn't require a warrant," he added by way of explanation.

"And, of course, you found nothing?" Holmes looked at him past the test tube he was holding up to the light.

"Not a blooming thing. I don't doubt that there had been arms there, since there were plenty of traces of oil on the floor. They explained the food away as being provisions for the soup kitchen they were about to set up for the local poor . . ."

"But the laboratory . . . ?" I said and could have bitten my tongue, for how could I have known about the laboratory unless . . .

Fortunately, Lestrade ignored my interruption. "As for all the test tubes and such, The Cain Foundation is apparently doing research into rickets and other diseases that affect the poor . . ."

"Yes," said Holmes, "and I have little doubt that—among many other things—that is precisely what they *are* doing. No, Lestrade, I'm afraid you will have to keep a round-the-clock surveillance on the premises. Use whatever pretext you need to, but let nothing and no one leave that building until we have determined what Cain intends to do with this hellish brew."

And then he explained to the Inspector what he had found.

"When this is over, Lestrade, I have no doubt that Watson and I will come quietly and plead guilty to breaking and entering . . ."

"I somehow doubt that it will come to that, Mr. 'Olmes," said Lestrade soberly. "What worries me is that this chap could strike anywhere and we've no idea where."

"Not *anywhere,* Lestrade. The man is an actor. He will want a theatrical effect, one that affects a number of people instantaneously. As long as he is immured in his so-called Church, we can deny him that possibility and frustrate him to the point where his *dementia* will drive him to reveal his purpose. Only one thing worries me . . ."

"And what is that, Holmes?" I interjected.

"He has promised London a Valentine and that promise runs out at midnight tonight."

Soon after, Lestrade left, gingerly clutching the test tube Holmes handed to him with instructions to have it further analysed in the police laboratories. None of us, however was in any real doubt as to what those tests would reveal.

It was also agreed that we should join the Inspector and his men in their Whitechapel vigil as this symbolic day drew to a close.

"And on the stroke of midnight we shall have Irene out of there, whether she will or no. There is no possible further purpose to be served by her remaining."

"Amen to that," I added fervently.

The rest of that day was the longest I can ever remember. There was nothing for us to do but wait.

Holmes pretended to occupy himself by doing some long-neglected filing of his Index books, while I occupied myself with a popular novel that had singularly failed to capture my attention for several weeks now and continued to do so today. Whenever I looked up, though, I noticed that his gaze was as much on the window as on the page.

Mrs. Hudson served us lunch but both of us picked at our food, much to the disgust of that good lady, who expressed herself by the way she rattled the crockery as she cleared it away.

In the afternoon I could stand the strain no longer and went for a walk into Regent's Park. How normal it all seemed, the soldiers strolling with their girls, the nannies with their small charges, elderly couples taking the air. All of them going about their daily business, quite unaware of what threat hung over their heads. And, for the life of me, had any one of them asked me to explain, I would have been totally lost for an explanation. Nonetheless, I was filled with a sense that somehow I was responsible— at least in part—for their continuing to enjoy the lives they took so much for granted.

Darkness had fallen when I arrived back at Baker Street and the gas lamps were shedding their familiar protective glow over the passers-by. As I climbed the stairs, I heard Mycroft's familiar booming tones.

"Sherlock," he was insisting, as I entered the room, "in the light of what you have told me, I do not see that we have any reasonable alternative. *Habeas corpus* may apply to normal circumstances but these are not normal circumstances. At least if the man is incarcerated in the Tower . . ."

"Then one of his minions would carry out

whatever is to be carried out and Cain will shout from the top of that Tower that he has been victimised for his beliefs. Governments have fallen for less."

It seems to me that Mycroft has lost several shades of his naturally ruddy complexion.

Holmes continued. "We must be constantly at his elbow and harass him until he commits himself to action. I am convinced that he means to act before this day is out. His ego will let him do no other. Lestrade and his men are in Whitechapel now and will remain there until further notice. Watson and I will be going there to join them shortly. Perhaps you would care to join us?"

The prospect did not seem to be one that exactly thrilled Mycroft but his answer was forestalled by a dramatic knock on the sitting-room door, which was then flung wide open.

In the doorway stood Oscar Wilde.

"My *Trois Mousquetaires*! Don't you adore Dumas? *Père*, of course, not *fils*. Lacks Balzac's rowdy canvas but what narrative drive! I knew I should find you all here and you shall not escape me. I have come to escort you to the experience of a lifetime . . ."

Then, seeing the blank expressions on three faces . . .

"The opening night of my new play, of course. I call it *The Importance of Being Earnest*. It is the ultimate embodiment of my philosophy of life that one must always take trivial things seriously and treat serious things with studied triviality. It is the only way to live."

Misreading our hesitation—for he had struck us all speechless—"No need to dress formally, my dears. It's just us. You shall be in my personal box."

It was Holmes who recovered first. "Mr. Wilde, I'm afraid . . ."

"Oscar, please. After all we have been through . . . !"

"Oscar, then. Much as we would like to, I'm afraid . . ."

Wilde covered one ear dramatically with a lavender-gloved hand. "I refuse to hear that tedious word 'No.' My nerves are already as taut as the strings of a Grecian lyre. I cannot believe that you would so much as contemplate leaving me to the unaccompanied company of that dreadful man, Cain. Why I invited him, I shall never know. Insane generosity will be my downfall, mark my words . . ."

"Did you say 'Cain'? But surely he will not be coming this evening?"

"Will he not? I ran into the appalling fellow and his cohorts just as I was leaving the theatre to come here. He has the box opposite ours. What he will make of my *bon mots*, Heaven knows. But, if we are fortunate, Heaven will not pass on what it knows to Mr. Cain."

He seemed prepared to go on in this extemporaneous vein indefinitely but my friend was not.

His face was set in that expression which spoke of absolute determination and boded ill for any adversary, the brows set over those hawk eyes. He positively bounded from his chair and hastened towards his bedroom. Turning at the doorway, he looked at Mycroft and myself.

"Come, gentlemen. Waterloo awaits. The question is—for whom?"

For once Wilde looked genuinely puzzled.

"Waterloo? You have been misinformed, Sherlock. The play is at the St. James's . . ."

CHAPTER FIFTEEN

As the cab drew near to the St. James's Theatre, a little to the south of Piccadilly Circus, we could see the crowds gathering and sense the excitement. Elegantly-dressed couples were descending from carriages. Others were standing outside the theatre, waiting for friends, bundled up against the freezing night air and hoping to draw warmth from the gas-lit torches that illuminated the building's façade.

It had started to snow earlier and the sky looked full of it. In fact, it turned into one of the worst blizzards the city had seen in years. It was most definitely a night for sitting by the fire with a warming drink. Instead, here we were traipsing around in pursuit of some wraith.

Mycroft turned to Wilde.

"Am I not correct in thinking that you have been making something of a habit of this lately?"

"Yes, I really must learn to restrain my literary productivity," Wilde replied. *"An Ideal Husband* at the Haymarket in January—though I fear its author falls somewhere short of its title—and now *Earnest.* I had better recline on my laurels for a while, lest London's actor-managers rebel against my dominance of their domain. But how wonderful to have a captive drawing-room of several hundred every evening to hear one talk—and have them pay for the privilege!"

As he spoke, he took a flower from his pocket and began to arrange it carefully in his buttonhole. It looked at first glance like a carnation—except that it was coloured *green*. Now it was Holmes who spoke.

"I have heard of your *penchant* for the green carnation on these occasions but, try as I may, I have been unable to deduce anything significant from it. Nature improved by art, perhaps? Pray set my poor mind at rest."

"As intelligent a supposition as I would have expected from you, Sherlock, and it will do as well as any," Wilde answered, adjusting the flower to his satisfaction. "In point of fact, its sole purpose is to irritate mine enemies. It means absolutely nothing at all—which I find to be its principal charm. But everyone *thinks* it does . . . Ah, what have we here?"

The cab had been approaching the Stage Door of the theatre and some sort of argument seemed to be taking place. The crowd of patrons were behaving as every English crowd behaves when it encounters a public incident—shying away, so as to stay uninvolved and yet lingering to satisfy its curiosity. This enabled us to see a middle-aged man in evening dress trying to thrust his way past a couple of burly policemen and get to the Stage Door.

The man's face was red with anger and he clutched a bouquet in one hand, presumably for one of the leading actresses. And then I saw that it was not a bouquet of flowers he carried but *vegetables*. There was a cauliflower surrounded by leeks, turnips, celery and carrots. It was as bizarre a spectacle as any I can remember.

Then the choleric man shouted at one of the policemen. "Don't you know who I am?"

"I'm afraid we know only too well, sir."

It was Wilde speaking in a subdued tone. As I looked at him, I could see that the incident had clearly affected him.

"That, gentlemen, is the Scarlet Marquess. Queensberry. Bosie's father," he added by way of explanation. "He believes that it is inappropriate for his son to be such—'good friends,' shall I say—with someone of my age and somewhat extravagant disposition. And there have been times lately . . ."—here he smiled wryly—"when I am forced to agree with him."

Then the old Wilde was back. The perverse buttonhole was firmly adjusted. "But one does not desert one's friends—*especially* when one strongly dislikes them. Driver, go on to the main entrance, if you please.

"I had hoped to introduce you to the remarkably talented cast who have the honour to be playing my little piece this evening. But perhaps later . . ."

A few moments later we were pushing our way through the theatre's crowded foyer.

It was clearly a gala occasion. I saw many a face famous from the society columns, a number of senior politicians from both parties . . . the great and the good and a number of others who would settle for being either. But now I was beginning to think as Wilde talked!

One thing it was impossible to miss was the way that every head turned as Wilde passed by. Many people spoke to him and for each of them he had a witty word, even though it seemed to me that the people he addressed were smiling even before he said anything, as if they *expected* it to be amusing. Many of them took a second look and whispered excitedly to their companions when they saw who else was in his party.

Then the lights briefly dimmed and the uniformed attendants started to discreetly urge the crowd towards the interior of the theatre, so that the performance could begin.

"Gentlemen, we are up here to the right," said Wilde. "Allow me to lead the way."

Just as we were on the point of following in his impressive wake, there was another altercation at the doors, which two attendants were trying to close.

Oh, no—not Queensberry again! I thought and my heart sank. The last thing we needed on this of all evenings was an irrelevant scene. We still had to locate Cain and his party, which was the whole point of coming here.

Then I saw that the cause of the argument was not an outraged aristocrat but a disreputable little boy. Wiggins!

With some difficulty I was able to disengage him from the clutches of one of the attendants, much to the astonishment of a few latecomers who were hurrying past. I led him to a corner of the foyer and then Holmes was at our side.

"What has happened, Wiggins?" I have never seen him more concerned.

"It's like this 'ere, Mr. 'Olmes," said the boy, trying to catch his breath and straighten his clothing at the same time—the latter being the more difficult of the two tasks, since it was not at all obvious what its original condition was meant to be.

"I was doing me regular rounds like I do every night and keeping an eye on that window, when the lady appears as usual. Only this time she seems kind of upset—frightened even. She usually just stands there for a bit, smoking her cigarette like, just to let me know she's all right. But tonight she was looking out for me and as soon as she sees me, she opens the window and throws me a package . . ."

"Where is the package?" I asked impatiently. But a true narrator with a story to tell must not be hurried.

"Then, just as I'm picking it up, I looks up at the window again and a couple of men have grabbed her and are trying to pull her away from the window. One of them's one of them undertaker fellers . . ."

"And the other?"

"Why, the one who calls 'is self Cain."

He then produced a small and by now grubby paper package from the recesses of his clothing and handed it to Holmes.

"So I reckoned I'd better get it to you toot sweet. I took a cab—and it wasn't no picnic, I can tell you. Had to break into that sovereign wot you gimme before the cabbie would take me. Then, when I got to Baker Street, Mrs. 'Udson told me where you was—so 'ere I am," he ended triumphantly.

"And you have done every bit as well as I would have expected, Wiggins," said Holmes, so warmly that the boy flushed with pleasure. "Watson, would you be kind enough to reimburse our colleague?" Then seeing the expression on my face—"I shall, of course, settle up with you later."

Now the theatre attendants, accustomed to recalcitrance in their patrons, were politely but firmly shepherding us towards Wilde's box, where Wilde and Mycroft were anxiously waiting. If they were surprised to see a street urchin added to their party, they hid it well.

At that moment the curtain rose.

I have to confess that my attention was totally divided. On the stage people seemed to be saying consistently witty things—if the laughter from the audience was anything to go by—while eating quantities of cucumber sandwiches. At the back of the box I could see Holmes and Wiggins, using what little light there was, poring over what looked like a map.

I don't know if you have ever had the experience but, when one has something on one's mind, everything you see, hear or read seems to refer to it, even though their context is quite different. It can be quite uncanny.

From what I could gather, several of the characters were pretending to be people they weren't and at one point one of the men, when asked to tell the pure and simple truth, said something like—"The truth is rarely pure and never simple."

If ever that applied to one of our cases, it applied to this one, I thought wryly. A mass murderer masquerading as a priest . . . an actress who became other people for a living and was now risking her life pretending to be a man . . . Holmes and his own disguises . . . even Wilde, using a foppish exterior to hide a brilliant mind. This line of speculation was starting to trigger another thought in my mind when . . .

. . . there was a thunder of applause as the first act ended and Wilde turned to us.

"Oh, *aren't* they performing well? I refer to the audience, of course . . ."

If he expected an answer, he was to be disappointed, for Mycroft and I were gathered round Holmes and the map. It appeared to be of London but it was no London that I knew. Instead of the familiar streets and landmarks, it consisted of a series of lines—some solid, some dotted—and a series of coloured circles from which the lines radiated.

Over to the right was a large square, the most prominent thing on the whole map.

"I think we can safely assume that, whatever the rest stands for, *this* . . ." and Holmes tapped the square with a bony forefinger—"represents the Church of the New Apocalypse. Which at least gives us our orientation. Now, that leaves us with these three other circles that are clearly indicated as the most important focus points of this network of lines, with *this* one . . ."—and he tapped the largest of the three that sat in the centre of the map—"as apparently the most important . . ."

I suppose, if I'm honest, I've always been inclined that way, but I find, as I get older, I often say things as they come into my head before I've entirely worked out their implications. On this occasion I heard myself saying—

"Hm, looks like a map of the Underground railway to me . . ."

"I think not, Doctor," Mycroft shook his head.

"I regret to say that after only ten years the network is not nearly as advanced as that. Next year Her Majesty's government hopes to electrify one of the lines but, alas . . ."

But Holmes interrupted his brother almost violently. These piercing eyes bored uncomfortably into mine.

"Say that again, Watson, if you please!"

"I said it reminds me of the Underground railway . . ."

Holmes leapt to his feet, almost knocking Wiggins over in the process.

"Not *railway*, old fellow. Not even Underground. But *under ground*. Oh, Watson, what a blind beetle I have been! The next time I seem to be getting above myself, I implore you to remind me of this evening.

"Don't you see, it all fits. You recall Porlock's clues? He said there were two . . ."

"One was his own name . . ."

"The 'person from Porlock.' Coleridge. The poem 'Kubla Khan' . . ." and Holmes began to recite . . .

"In Xanadu did Kubla Khan
A stately pleasure dome decree . . .

"And that is as far as we went, Watson. I foolishly thought it referred to the Church. But the verse continues . . .

"Where Alph, the sacred river, ran
Through caverns measureless to man
Down to a sunless sea . . ."

"But, Holmes, I still . . ."

"Bear with me, Watson. Porlock's second clue?"

"Remember Musgrave."

"Something I shall hardly care to do, now that I have made the identical mistake twice! You will remember the piece of doggerel I quoted to you—the Musgrave Ritual?"

"Indeed."

"When I first encountered it, I followed its instructions to the letter and number—and it took me precisely nowhere. Except literally to a blank wall. For the simple reason that I had ignored the three little words that were the key to the whole puzzle—just as I have ignored them in this case . . ."

"And they were?"

" 'And so under.' I was standing on top of the solution to the problem which was literally 'under' my feet. As it is in this case—under all our feet. Gentlemen . . ."—he flourished the map—"I will stake what is left of my reputation that what we are looking at is a map of the London sewer system."

There was a moment of stunned silence in the box. All I could hear was the subdued and cheerful background noise of the theatre audience, as they waited for Wilde's play to recommence.

Then Holmes said heavily, looking at none of us—"And, of course, it tells us all we need to know about one old, vexed question . . .

"The Ripper. This was how he could appear and disappear at will in the midst of Whitechapel and, later, anywhere he chose. He had his own private highway."

It suddenly came to me. "The Opera!"

"Precisely, old fellow. That sound of a metal door closing. Only it wasn't a door at all, except figuratively. It was a metal cover over a manhole. While we were busy banging doors and kicking walls, our friend was lurking inches beneath our very feet and laughing at our puny efforts."

"But, Holmes, what is the significance of the map now and why did Irene think it so important to get it to us that she gave herself away. My God, Holmes, that poor woman! We must . . ."

"And we shall, old friend, never fear. Cain's men have Irene—for the moment—but we have the map and we have Cain. As long as he is in our sights, he can hardly bring War, Famine, Death or, indeed, Pestilence upon this great city, for there is no way that he will delegate that power to underlings. His God has given the power to him alone and it must be by *his* hand . . ."

All our eyes turned to the box immediately opposite ours, where Cain and his entourage had remained throughout. I reached for a pair of opera glasses but, just as I did so, the house lights dimmed for the start of the second act.

Once again, some of Wilde's lines seemed to carry an additional, sometimes surrealistic, resonance for me.

"I hope you have not been living a double life," one of the young ladies accuses the object of her affection, "pretending to be wicked and being really good all the time. That would be hypocrisy." The opposition of Good versus Evil and the ability to identify which was which was at the very heart of the affair we were trying to untangle.

Throughout the rest of the act there were two sets of dialogue competing for my attention, for just behind me Holmes was still poring over the map and muttering to himself—"Something more, something more."

If I'm honest, there were *three* strands of thought taxing my poor brain. Something I had heard this evening that didn't make sense. Slowly it was coming back to me—something to do with Cain.

And I was obviously not the only one whose mind had been working in parallel, for, as the curtain descended once more to even greater applause, Mycroft leaned across to his brother.

"May I look at that map again?"

Having done so, he raised his eyes to ours and said in a voice as cold as any I have ever heard . . .

"This is not merely a map of the London sewer system. It is overlaid with a map of the city's water supply. You can see the conduits and the aqueducts quite clearly. This maniac means to poison London's drinking water."

At which point I remembered Holmes's experiments that showed how the chemical we had removed from Cain's church behaved in water. If Mycroft was right, thousands—perhaps millions would die.

And then the other thing came to me.

"Wiggins," I said, "you saw Cain seizing Miss Adler at what time?"

"Seven o'clock, Doctor. I'm always outside that there window at seven on the dot."

"And yet you, Mr. Wilde, told us that you saw Cain arrive here at the theatre well before you left to collect us? At what time?"

Wilde did not hesitate.

"Naturally, I have been here most of the day *pour encourager les autres*. Cain and Co. arrived, as large as life and twice as ugly, no later than six-thirty."

"So," I said, "there are either identical twin Cains or . . ."

"One of them is *not* Cain," said Holmes in the

silence that followed. "Watson, I declare I never get your limits."

He carefully folded the map and thrust it into an inside pocket, as he rose to his feet.

"And now, gentlemen, I suggest we put Watson's theory to the test."

As quickly as we could without drawing undue attention to ourselves, we left the box and moved around the perimeter of the auditorium to the opposite side, where an identical staircase took us up to the box opposite ours.

Here it was Wilde who took the initiative. Knocking on the door, he stepped smartly inside.

"My dear Cain, I could not resist coming over to ask you how you and your friends are enjoying my little *soufflé*. It is written by a butterfly for butterflies. But you, I suspect, are more like blowflies . . ."

Cain and his two companions had risen to their feet in surprise at Wilde's intrusion and the box was now decidedly crowded. Which was perhaps why none of us anticipated what happened next.

Holmes reached past the bulk of Wilde and grasped Cain's long blond beard. A moment later he was holding a large tuft of it in his hand. The rest of it was hanging lopsidedly from the face of a man who was most decidedly not Janus Cain.

"If I may recommend Leichner's patent fixative in future, my dear fellow. Far more effective

228

and considerably less painful to remove."

"Wiggins. Go and fetch the Manager. Mr. Holmes's compliments and he needs to see him right away."

The boy scuttled off and was back in moments with an impressive and portly man in tails, who looked both surprised and concerned by the sight that greeted him. However, a few words from Mycroft, whom he clearly recognised, and Wilde soon achieved the desired result. He agreed to lock our "prisoners" in their box and have his men stand guard until the police arrived.

As the key turned in the lock, I heard Wilde call out to them.

"Now, I particularly want you to notice the *dénouement*, since I find it particularly ingenious. But I mustn't give the plot away . . ."

As the third and final act began, Holmes, Mycroft, Wilde and I stood in the Stalls bar. Apart from a barman clearing glasses, we had the place to ourselves and were able to spread the map out, so that we could examine it properly.

Wiggins had reluctantly been sent off to Whitechapel with a note from Holmes to Lestrade. His disappointment at missing "the exciting part," as he called it, was somewhat alleviated by the prospect of the second cab ride in one day and the feel of the additional sovereign warming the palm of his grubby little hand.

Now that we could see the map in good light, it was clear that Mycroft was right. The sewer system was certainly the means but the end—marked with the coloured circles—was a handful of junction points dotted over the map.

"It has long been a matter of contention and controversy in certain circles," Mycroft explained, "that the conduits for the city's water supply should lie in such close proximity to its sewers. The excuse has always been that—apart from the huge capital cost of providing an alternative and the concomitant burden on the taxpayer—the present system offered convenience. The access provided by the sewer network made it relatively easy to monitor the water supply . . ."

"Or, equally, to tamper with it," Holmes added grimly. "You need not explain that aspect further, Mycroft. I am fully persuaded. And I am equally persuaded that Cain still means to carry out his plan before this day is over. Can you, with your apparently infinite knowledge of London's intestinal system, suggest where Cain is likely to strike? Is there a vulnerable 'heart' somewhere in these intestines?"

"Undoubtedly. And it is not far from here . . ."

He placed an enormous finger on the largest circle.

"This spot represents the conflux of several streams. It was chosen originally because it happened to be the bed of an underground river that, before it was diverted, ran into the Thames . . ."

"*Through caverns measureless to man. Down to a sunless sea.*" Holmes spoke as if to himself.

"Many of us have argued that electing to focus so many key resources on a site so close to the main concentration of population was strategically unsound but, as I say, for budgetary reasons . . ."

"I think we may safely assume that with his access to every shade of official opinion, Daintry—and now Cain—has done his homework and could probably add a few footnotes for even you, Mycroft."

He consulted his watch.

"Ten-thirty. We have not a moment to lose. Mycroft, may I suggest you go to Whitechapel and strengthen Lestrade's resolve to investigate that Church, paying particular attention this time to its cellars? Not that I have any doubts about the good Inspector. What he may lack in intelligence he more than makes up for in courage and determination. He will take the rats and shake them."

He turned to Wilde.

"Oscar,"—and this time there was genuine warmth in his use of Wilde's christian name— "your help has been immeasurable. May I wish you every success—not only with tonight's play but with any other dramas you may be going through?"

Wilde did not miss Holmes's change of tone and it was clear he was moved by it but a second later the showman was in charge again.

"Sherlock, how can you possibly expect me, the leading dramatist of my age, a man who has enriched and ennobled every literary form that I have touched, to miss the last act of this tawdry entertainment? I shall accompany you to the Gates of Hell, if need be."

"But won't your audience expect you to appear on stage at the end of the play?" I asked.

"They may, they very well may," he replied, "but I shall not take a call tonight. One feels so much like a German band."

I could not be sure but I thought Holmes seemed positively glad that he had lost the argument.

He looked at the map for the last time and placed his finger where his brother's had been.

"And so, gentlemen, we meet at Philippi. The question is . . ."—and he looked up at Mycroft—"exactly where *is* Philippi?"

"Trafalgar Square."

CHAPTER SIXTEEN

In the more than fifty years he has stood there Nelson can hardly have looked down on a more bizarre spectacle—not even on the rowdiest Boat Race Night—as a cordon of police restrained curious onlookers, while three well-dressed middle-aged gentlemen lowered themselves gingerly into the bowels of the earth in the middle of Trafalgar Square. For once the pigeons really did have something to coo about.

While we had been in the theatre, it had begun to snow even harder. The Square looked like a belated Christmas card and Landseer's famous lions lay huddled under a white blanket. The only touch of black was the yawning hole at our feet.

Somehow I had envisioned having to climb down some vertiginous ladder but, in fact, we encountered a rather elaborate circular metal staircase that wound down into blackness. Being totally unprepared for such a safari, we had nothing but the clothes we stood in but Holmes had had the foresight to borrow the lanterns from two of the policemen. If they were surprised by our actions, they hid it well. Holmes, I could see, was quite touched when the sergeant saluted and said—

"Glad to be of service, Mr. Holmes. *You've* helped *us* often enough."

Now the beams guided our descent until we found ourselves on a sort of half-landing, which held a substantial locker. This was clearly where the inspectors kept their equipment and it held two much larger lanterns, which were well-trimmed and we soon had them burning brightly.

At last we could see something of our surroundings and Wilde's fanciful description of the Gates of Hell suddenly did not seem so far amiss.

We were in a cavern which, if not measureless to man, was certainly of significant size. It was like an enclosed canal with a narrow footpath running along one side of a rushing stream. By some trick of sensory balance—which I have no doubt Holmes could easily explain—now that we could actually see the rushing waters, they somehow seemed louder. What had been a subdued background noise in the dark now became a roar. While not a torrent, we were looking at more of a river than a stream.

Holmes raised his lantern above his head.

"Up there!" he cried over the din.

As I followed his pointing finger, I could now see a series of pipes running parallel to the flood and a few feet higher. Some few yards upstream was another of the metal landings. Several steps led up to it and it was enclosed with a handrail.

"Presumably that is the inspection platform," said Holmes. "I assume that is where the water supply is routinely tested. I suggest we take a closer look."

"If it's all the same to you, gentlemen, I think I'll look from here."

Wilde was looking decidedly green, as far as once could tell in the flickering light of the lanterns. And, indeed, the air in the cavern was far from pleasant.

"I think I may have just discovered," he added weakly, "that I suffer from both vertigo *and* claustrophobia. Regard me as waiting in the wings and listening for my cue."

Holmes and I continued our descent until we set foot on the path and began to move carefully towards the inspection platform. The path itself was no more than eighteen inches wide and below us was "Alph, the sacred river" or— as it seemed to me—London's equivalent of the Styx.

We soon reached the platform and Holmes was on it in a trice. I could see him examining an array of valves, levers and hatches and then he turned in my direction.

"Good news, old fellow. According to Mycroft, these stations are examined quarterly. This machinery has had time to gather dust and no one has disturbed it recently. Cain has not been here yet."

"Thank heaven we are in time," I said, breathing a distinct sight of relief.

Then I saw Holmes look over my shoulder and gaze upstream. The light from the lantern was reflected from an expression I knew so well. Half tense, half excited, it was the look that invariably came over him when an affair was reaching its crisis.

"Yes, Watson, we are in time—but for what, I wonder?"

I turned to follow his gaze and there, where the river curved before coming to meet us, I distinctly saw the reflection of light on the ceiling of the tunnel. We were no longer the only denizens of this hellish terrain. It was a scene from Dante's *Inferno*.

"Quick, Watson, I seem to remember we passed a small embrasure some few yards back . . ."

A few moments later we were hidden in a shallow space beside a pile of equipment, on the purpose of which I did not even wish to speculate. Fortunately, our lanterns were of the "dark" variety and we were able to cover the flames, so that they would not give away our presence.

By this time the light on the roof of the cavern was growing steadily brighter and then . . . around the bend towards us came a small boat!

It was a small skiff being rowed by one of Cain's men in black. His back was naturally towards us but over his shoulder, seated in the stern was Janus Cain—and Irene Adler.

Irene was still wearing her male attire but her blonde hair was flowing free around her face. It was clear from the way she was sitting, with Cain's arm loosely draped around her shoulder, that her hands at least were bound.

If she was frightened, it did not show. Rather, her jaw was set in anger and frustration and her eyes flashed fury. I reflected that Cain was wise to protect himself from the hands of any woman in this mood, let alone a woman of Irene's strength of purpose.

Now the boat bumped against the side and I could see the oarsman slip a rope through an iron ring embedded in the stone. This was obviously the way the sewer workers transported their heavier equipment.

As he steadied the boat, Cain stepped catlike on to the path and pulled an unwilling Irene up beside him.

"Thank God the swine hasn't hurt her," I whispered in Holmes's ear.

And then Cain did the last thing I could have expected . . .

He spoke to us.

"Good evening, Sherlock Holmes. For I have no doubt you are there in the gloom. When those predictable policemen broke into the Church, I assumed that you had divined my purpose. Too late, alas, as you were last time. Nonetheless, I must mark you top of the class. Why don't you come out into the light where we can see one another?"

As Cain spoke, he was maneouvring himself up the steps and on to the inspection platform, pulling a reluctant Irene with him and using her body as a shield.

"I shall be glad to join you, Cain," Holmes called back, bending to adjust the flame in the lantern. "It is only fitting this thing should end with just the two of us."

Then to me in the softest undertones.

"Stay where you are, old fellow. I assume you have . . . ?"

"You may depend on it Holmes." It is a long time since I have accompanied him on an adventure such as this without my trusty service revolver. As we have often discovered, an Eley's No. 2 is an excellent argument in any situation.

With that, Holmes raised his lantern above his head and stepped out into the light.

Cain seemed a trifle surprised.

"So the Forces of Good are dispersed this evening, doubtless waiting in the wrong place, as usual? Ah well, it is of little matter. My own contribution will more than suffice to set the process in train . . ."

At this he took from an inner pocket one of the phials that Holmes had abstracted earlier from the Whitechapel laboratory. Without ever quite

238

taking his eye off Holmes, he looked at it almost lovingly.

"May I introduce you to Pestilence—the First Horseman . . . or perhaps, in the light of our present circumstances, I should say, Boatman . . . of the New Apocalypse. This will give the deluded citizens of that Sodom and Gomorrah you call London a taste—if you will pardon my jest—of what my God has in store for them.

"Where Pestilence goes . . ."—and now his voice was rising in pitch—"Death will follow. As the populace dies, those that are left will revert to their primitive state and fight over such tainted food as they can find. That will bring Famine and War and, yet again, Death."

"And what of you and your followers?" Holmes was humouring the man or buying time—or both. "How will *you* escape the Four Horsemen?"

"My followers . . . ?" Cain sounded almost wistful. "Sadly, they no longer will be among the chosen few to be saved. In the Church I had made provision for them but you and your cohorts—with your impertinent intrusion—have condemned them to share your fate. Since the Lord has made me all-seeing, I have, of course, prepared an alternative contingency that will suffice for my lady and myself. We shall immure ourselves in a degree of luxury until the holocaust is past and we can re-emerge to take up our rightful place on the throne of a new order . . ."

"But it was *Irene* who betrayed you, Daintry. She is unworthy to sit at your right hand."

For a moment I was shocked, until I realised Holmes's tactic. He was deliberately splintering the man's delusion at his moment of greatest stress. Was he Daintry or Cain. Was Irene Adler his idol or his enemy? Even in the dim light I could see the jumble of emotions contort his face, as he struggled for control.

"Irene!" he cried in the voice of one who has lost his dearest possession. The sound echoed up and down that dank space.

"No, never *Irene*. Violetta, perhaps. Or Senta. Or that boy, Ned you sent to spy on me. Or someone else. But never Irene . . . I have known for years that she was my destiny . . . No, stay precisely where you are . . ."

Holmes had slowly moved a few paces closer to the couple and it was this that broke the spell. A look of animal cunning replaced the abstract expression on Cain's face and he pulled Irene closer to him.

"You are a clever fiend, Sherlock Holmes, but not clever enough. Nothing must stand in the way of God's Purpose—not even Irene. But, unless you choose to act foolishly, it will not come to that. I have one small task to accomplish and then we shall be on our way. Irene will come to understand and share that Purpose. Incidentally, you will both see and observe that my loyal assistant, Sugarman has his pistol trained on you. Now, if you will excuse me one moment . . ."

Cain pulled Irene awkwardly towards the control panel. Clearly, he had familiarised himself with the way things worked and I had visions of him alone down here at dead of night poring over the various dials and taps. If so, he had never had to practice with a determined woman to control.

As he reached out one arm and opened a valve, he held on to Irene with the other—the one that held the phial. Then everything happened in a blur . . .

With her hands tied behind her back, Irene did what only a woman would think of doing. She bent forward towards the restraining arm—and *bit* it!

Cain's reaction was purely instinctive. He gave a cry of pain, his arm jerked up and away from his body . . . and the lethal phial flew up and up into the air, turning and twisting as it went.

Then I heard Holmes shout—"*Now,* Watson!"— and I saw that Sugarman had his pistol raised to fire. In that split second all the events of the last few days . . . all the horror of those old cold-blooded killings of helpless women . . . the danger Irene had undergone and the bravery she had shown . . . the sheer callousness—no, the evil—that was Cain . . . all of this flashed through my mind, as I stepped out of the shadow

241

with my revolver cocked. To me that black figure in the boat might as well have been an Afghan tribesman at Maiwand. He was simply the enemy.

I have never shot better in my life. The bullet took him in the shoulder. His gun dropped from his paralysed fingers into the depths and he sank to the bottom of the boat.

Only then did I remember the phial. We had saved the water supply but heaven knew what would happen if that hell brew further contaminated the sewers.

I looked up and saw it relentlessly descending, catching the fitful light on its glass surface as it did so.

And then a hand plucked it out of thin air and held it aloft like Arthur brandishing Excalibur.

"I rather regret that I am too old to play cricket for England," said Oscar Wilde. "I remember when I was up at Oxford watching them practise in the Parks. There was one bowler whose left leg was a Greek poem . . ."

I turned my attention back to the rest of the scenario, where several things seemed to happen at once.

Sugarman had clearly not tied up the boat too securely—or perhaps he had been in the process of untying it, ready for departure when my bullet struck him. In any event the painter had worked itself loose and Cain's means of escape was drifting steadily away from the bank.

For the moment it took all his attention. Seeing him distracted, Holmes closed the intervening gap and snatched Irene from the platform.

"Watson!" he cried urgently, and in no time I was beside them and leading her to safety.

Seeing what had happened, Cain gave a scream of frustration such as I have never heard from a human throat. Then I saw his face. The black eyes were like two holes leading straight to Hell and the man was smiling—if one could call something so feral a smile. The lips were drawn back from the teeth and the skin was taut on his skull. I was looking at a living death's head.

He stood on the platform looking down at the man who had finally thwarted all his plans. Then he threw himself down at Holmes.

Silently they wrestled on the brink of this infernal maelstrom. I had not realised how fast it was flowing until I saw how far the boat had already drifted. It was now well out of reach. Nor had I realised quite how many currents and eddies disturbed its oily surface.

Another vision came to me as the two men struggled for supremacy.

It was an encounter I had not witnessed but which I had played through in my mind more times than I cared to recall. It was of Holmes and Moriarty locked in deadly embrace on a mountain path, while the deadly Reichenbach Falls seethed below, waiting to claim either or both of them.

To and fro they struggled, evenly matched, neither giving an inch.

And then my heart almost stopped, for Cain managed to wrench one hand free and pulled something from his pocket that caught the light. It was an open razor.

The sight of it had quite the opposite effect on Holmes than his opponent can have expected.

"It seems that your God has deserted you after all and you are once again the same pathetic creature you were when you butchered those lost souls all those years ago. Then your peers saw fit to let you go free and undoubtedly would again to save their own faces. But I am *not* your peer, Daintry. You sent those women to meet their Maker. I think it is now time for you to meet yours . . ."

And with a lightning move learned from *baritsu*, Holmes hooked his foot behind Cain's leg and threw his whole weight against it.

Without even a cry Cain dropped headfirst into the torrent hitting it like a dead weight. He did not appear again. In falling, he must have impaled himself on his razor, for a bright ribbon of blood floated to the surface and extended like a painter's first tentative brush stroke. Beyond it all that was to be seen was the boat floating aimlessly, until it disappeared around the next bend.

CHAPTER SEVENTEEN

It was well past midnight and we were once again sitting in the Café Royal.

Our reappearance from the depths of Trafalgar Square had caused, if possible, even more of a stir than our entry. Two dishevelled men leading a girl dressed as a boy and the unmistakable figure of Oscar Wilde proudly brandishing a test tube was not an everyday sight.

Once safely back on the surface, however, the rest of us seemed to succumb to a sense of anti-climax—but not Wilde. Here was a drama that—yes, he had to admit it—rivalled anything even he had so far conceived. Champagne was called for, vintage champagne, and he would provide it.

The Café Royal was close by and did not turn a hair as one of their best customers arrive with his motley band. A private room was provided and, by that alchemy only the finest establishments can achieve, the necessary toilet items were procured to enable Irene to effect a re-transformation to the beautiful woman who belonged in such a setting.

Before leaving Trafalgar Square Holmes had dispatched one of the constables to Whitechapel and before long the door of the room opened to admit both Mycroft and Lestrade, looking as much the worse for wear as we felt.

Bone weary but essentially happy, we raised our glasses—filled with Wilde's excellent champagne—in a silent toast. Precisely what we were toasting I am not quite sure. To the continuance of life as we know it, perhaps. To the fact that the millions sleeping peacefully all over London would never know how close they had come to Armageddon.

Holmes, as ever, was anxious to tie up loose ends. Having briefly narrated our own adventures, he urged Lestrade to tell us what had transpired at Whitechapel.

"Oh, I think we can safely say that everything there is now tickety-boo, Mr. 'Olmes. As a matter of fact, I'm pretty sure they knew the game was up even before we broke in. Apart from the workers, there was hardly anybody left there. Those fellers in black had made a run for it. I couldn't understand it at first because we'd had the place surrounded all day and made our presence known. But when Mr. Mycroft arrived, then the penny dropped, so to speak. They must have nipped through the sewers, too. Good luck to them, say I.

"We'd been on top of the problem all the time—if you'll pardon the pun. All the stuff that had vanished was in the cellars and those had been bricked over. I say 'was,' because it's now under lock and key at the Yard. Enough to start a small war there . . ."

"Which was precisely what Cain had in mind," Holmes interjected bleakly. "And what about the chemicals?"

"Got all those, too. Though we nearly had a little accident there. When I told young McLinsky what we were dealing with, do you know what he said?"

"Enlighten us, Lestrade," I said, knowing we should hear anyway.

" 'Shall I pour it down the drain, Inspector?' "

Even though we had all heard more humorous stories, the laughter in the room served as a vent for our feelings.

When it had died down, Mycroft got to his feet and raised his glass.

"I think I may say that we have tonight concluded an episode which may never find a place in the official history books but which will, nonetheless, prove to have played a part in safeguarding the future of this island race. On behalf of Her Majesty's Government, gentlemen—and lady—I thank you!"

And then an unfamiliar Oscar Wilde responded.

Although the foppish dress remained, the manner was gone. His eyes were bright and his voice low, as he said—

"I find sincerity a little frightening, I must confess. Which, I suppose, is why I take such pains to hide from it in public. I am tempted to say that tonight proves the importance of being Oscar—but for once I shall resist temptation. In these last few days I have witnessed loyalty, courage and every kind of love . . ." Did I sense his eyes linger on Holmes and Irene?—"It has made me feel humble. And may I tell you something . . . ? I *like* the feeling . . . in small doses!"

Then it was as if everything that was to be said had been said. Gradually the room emptied. Lestrade buttoned officialdom round him like a cloak and returned to the Yard to check on the latest developments from Whitechapel and—I strongly suspected—to tell everyone how he had masterminded another *coup*—with a little help from that consulting detective fellow . . . what was his name? . . . in Baker Street.

Mycroft with a touching old world gallantry—insisting on escorting Irene back to Covent Garden, stressing that it was, in reality, on his way back to Pall Mall.

As she left, Irene went up to Holmes. She said not a word but gently put both arms around him and for a moment laid her head on his shoulder. The rest of us busied ourselves collecting our bits and pieces preparatory to departing. Then she took Mycroft's arm and hurried out of the room.

Wilde was the last to leave. He rose to his feet,

still holding his glass and raised it to Holmes and myself.

"Gentlemen, my sense of theatre tells me that it is time for the captains to depart and leave the stage to the kings. If I had not made it an immutable rule to treat all things serious with studied triviality, I would thank you, but as it is . . ."

For the first time since we had known him—and possibly for the first time in his life—Wilde seemed lost for words.

Holmes made good the deficit by walking over to him and holding out his hand. The two men shook hands with a quiet formality that I personally found touching. Then Wilde left the room.

"Well, Watson?"

"Well, Holmes?"

"We have shared a few untoward adventures these last few years, old friend, but none, I think, in which more was at stake. Although I pray they will not come to know of it, never have so many owed so much to so few . . ."

"Why, Holmes, that is almost poetic. I must make a note of it for the day when I write the case up."

"At which time you will undoubtedly introduce your customary element of the romantic and reduce the role played by logic and deduction."

But for once his tone carried little conviction.

He swirled the remains of the champagne in his glass and appeared to look for something in its depths that he did not find there.

"The human mind is a disturbing thing, Watson. One moment it is capable of devising something that will benefit its fellow man—improve his lot in life or alleviate suffering for millions. The next it can focus on obliterating those same people. Even a single mind housed in one fragile person, is capable of swinging like a pendulum between Good and Evil for no apparent reason.

"Sometimes I see that little creature we call the soul lost in a maze, bruising itself on the ungiving walls of that maze, as it seeks the right path . . ."

"But surely, Holmes, it has always been thus?"

"I suppose you are right, old fellow, but we live in times where the old order is changing faster than at any time in the history of mankind. There was a time when a man of learning could know all there was to know. That time is long past and will not come again. Events are changing faster than man can adapt to that change—that is my concern.

"Was the evil in Cain innate or did the means to give form to that evil help create it and encourage it. Is the progress we talk about so blithely necessarily a help to improving our lot—or might it turn out to be more of a hindrance? And since none of us can turn back the clock, then where are we heading?"

Then he looked up full into my face.

"Of one thing I am certain, old friend. Whatever it portends for generations yet unborn, we, fortunately, shall not be here to see it or have it upset the even tenor of our ways.

"And now I do believe we have earned our beds."

With that, he did something quite untypical. He took his empty champagne glass and hurled it ritualistically into the fireplace. A moment later I found myself doing the same.

The next morning I confess I slept in but, as she served me my breakfast, Mrs. Hudson informed me that Holmes had left her instructions not to disturb him until he woke of his own accord. I was not surprised to hear it. After periods of intense activity it was not uncommon for him to sleep for a day or two at a time and I could think of no case where the tension had been greater or more sustained.

I sat with my second cup of tea and read the glowing reviews of Wilde's play.

In *The World* William Archer reported that he had "sent wave after wave of laughter curling and foaming round the theatre," while the critic from *The New York Times* was of the opinion that "Oscar Wilde may be said to have at last, and by a single stroke, put his enemies under his feet." I found myself with an odd feeling that this latter verdict might be tempting providence.

Then there was a discreet cough and Mrs. Hudson announced that I had a visitor

"Don't you mean *Holmes* has a visitor?"

"No, Doctor. The lady made sure Mr. Holmes was *not* available before she would come in. She particularly wants to see *you,* Doctor."

And a moment later Irene Adler walked through the door. This was the Irene I had first met when this whole affair began—could it be just a few short days ago? It was as though the events of the night before had never happened. The woman looked like a fashion plate in the identical outfit she had worn for our lunch at Rules before our world had been turned upside down.

Even so, I could sense that her composure was only on the surface. Even though she carried herself like the actress she was, something was most definitely on her mind.

That clear, level gaze met mine for a moment, then she looked away.

"I have come to say goodbye."

Having made the initial statement, she seemed to gain in confidence and looked at me again, as though she knew I would understand what was going through her mind.

"After all that has happened, London can never be the same for me. So many things . . ." her eyes flickered over Holmes's armchair and away— ". . . so many things . . ."

"But perhaps the most important thing is that I have been forced to look at the direction of my life these past few years. John, I have been drifting—I see that now. But there must be an end to drifting. It is time to go back and find my roots and I know now that they are in America—not here.

"For good or ill, I am a woman who knows her mind and this morning she made that mind up. I have just come from the Cunard office and I sail from Southampton tomorrow morning on the S.S. *Lucania* for New York . . ."

"New York?"

"Yes, New York. Surely you would not wish New *Jersey* on me again?" For a moment she was almost mischievous.

"They say it has come on by leaps and bounds lately. And—who knows?—they may need a stand-in at the Met. Although I shall stay well away from the cellars!

"Dear John, you are so understanding. I only wish we had had more time to laugh as we did that day at Rules. I don't know if you noticed but I stole the menu. I shall have it framed, so that I can remember . . . The Three Musketeers."

She took my hand in hers, pressed it gently, then stretched on tiptoe to kiss my cheek.

At the door she turned.

"Say goodbye to your friend for me, please. And tell him Irene Adler says 'Thank you.'

You see, John, for a very long time now, for me Sherlock Holmes has always been *the* man . . ."

And then she was gone.

The next morning over breakfast Holmes looked up and said—

"Watson, I think we owe ourselves a holiday. Why should the criminal fraternity of London have us all to themselves. What would you say, my dear fellow, to a trip to—say—New York?"

As he got up and went over to the mantelpiece to fill his pipe, I picked up the newspaper he had been reading. It was folded so that the only item to be read was the one concerning shipping movements. I noticed that the S.S. *Lucania* had sailed for New York on the morning tide.

Books are produced
in the United States
using U.S.-based
materials

Books are printed
using a revolutionary
new process called
THINKtech™ that
lowers energy usage
by 70% and increases
overall quality

Books are durable
and flexible because
of smythe-sewing

Paper is sourced
using environmentally
responsible foresting
methods and the
paper is acid-free

Center Point Large Print
600 Brooks Road / PO Box 1
Thorndike, ME 04986-0001 USA

(207) 568-3717

US & Canada:
1 800 929-9108
www.centerpointlargeprint.com